THE AERIAL LETTER

THE AERIAL LETTER

Nicole Brossard

Translated
by

MARLENE WILDEMAN

The
Women's
Press

CANADIAN CATALOGUING IN PUBLICATION DATA

Brossard, Nicole, 1943-
The aerial letter

Translation of: La lettre aerienne.
ISBN 0-88961-123-8

1. Women. 2. Lesbianism 3. Patriarchy.
I. Title.

HQ1208.B7613 1988   305.4   C88-093723-8

Originally published in French
as *La Lettre aérienne*
by Les Editions du remue-ménage,
Montreal, 1985

Copyright © 1988 Marlene Wildeman

Cover photograph "La Fontaine des naïades," P. Marton
Cover design: Liz Martin
Revision and editing: Wendy Waring
Copy editor: Margaret Christakos

Printed and bound in Canada

Published by
The Women's Press
229 College Street No. 204
Toronto, Ontario M5T 1R4

This book was produced by
the collective effort of The Women's Press.
This book was the project of
the Translation Group.

The Women's Press gratefully acknowledges
financial support from The Canada Council
and the Ontario Arts Council

CONTENTS

ERRANT AND AIR-BORN
IN THE CITY

The origin is not the mother, but the sense I give to
words, and, originally I am a woman.

> Nicole Brossard, *The Aerial Letter*,
> tr. Marlene Wildeman, p. 111

this book is primarily concerned with the mind / spirit /
body pollution inflicted through patriarchal myth and
language .... Phallic myth and language generate, legitimate, and mask the material pollution that threatens to
terminate all sentient life on this planet.

> Mary Daly, *Gyn/Ecology*.
> *The Metaethics of Radical Feminism*, p. 9

Les lettres ... sont comme une pulsation qui naît et se
propage dans la continuité de la tradition littéraire de la
culture des femmes.

> Jovette Marchessault,
> *La Saga des poules mouillées*[1]

A friend said to me with considerable fervour that she had
read *La Lettre aérienne* and had *loved* it. Such a strong emotional response to a book of theory may seem strange, and yet
I too have read and loved these texts. Their extraordinary texture and the zany peregrinations of the words have brought
me pleasure, insight and joy; they offered me warm complicity. Like Nicole Brossard, *"I want* in fact *to see women's form
taking shape in the trajectory of the species"* (p. 65). I hope that
many more English-speaking readers will now discover with
pleasure how deeply and intimately Brossard's texts touch the

9

feelings, sparking thought and strengthening their conviction that change is possible. After reading these texts, perhaps the reader will recognize, for the first time, vital things about herself and society. She will surely recognize herself as a strong and articulate woman in a context of the wholeness and integrity of human experience. She may be filled with healthy anger against dominant social practices. Brossard uses words such as "complicity," "coincidence," "synchrony," "appreciation" to express that exciting sense of being on the same wavelength as other active feminists. I am particularly grateful to Brossard for the way in which her writing has put me in touch with myself. I am equally grateful for the way in which she has helped me to see more clearly how conventions of patriarchy make things work the way they do, as well as to see what we can do together to make them work differently.

The first signs of modern feminism in Quebec occurred in the late 1960s. Since that time the feminist movement has retained a broad base and vitality. Its particularly strong energy has come from angry reaction against the images, myths and roles imposed on women in traditional Quebec society. The writers and activists who produced Quebec feminism in all its uniqueness have done an analysis which forces people to see social practices clearly, while revealing hidden patterns, assumptions and ideologies. This is a multi-faceted, probing analysis which is valid and helpful in understanding the situation not only in Quebec but everywhere else in Canada and the Western world. With this analysis has come an astonishing body of poetry, prose, drama and essays, in which imagination and creative power are used both to subvert the codes and conventions of dominant discourse and to give form to an alternative vision of human society.

Part of the uniqueness of that vision comes from the fact that Quebec feminists with extraordinary insight seized the opportunity to work at a certain intellectual crossroads where challenging questions proposed new paths for exploration.

During the Quiet Revolution in Quebec, the transformation of European thought by new trends in philosophy, psychoanalysis, and linguistics, the rise of the counter-culture in the United States, and modernity in Quebec all offered a radical challenge to dominant ideologies through their critique of language and power. Such initiatives proved useful to Quebec feminists, although they were not deluded by the sexist nature of these streams of thought. These women chose what they could use and made an original synthesis of ideas. While clearing this radical and creative path, Quebec feminists also followed with interest and drew great encouragement from strong feminist movements in France and the United States.

Nicole Brossard, Quebec's leading feminist writer, perceived very early the importance of exploring all these directions simultaneously. At her disposal was an approach to writing, techniques for analysis, and elements of a world view which together would allow her to to issue a major challenge to the epistemologies and the ontological assumptions of dominant culture. She began her writing career as a poet, whose inner space was filled with the image of a new dawn: "At dawn, our spirit is extravagant; it wanders freely in forbidden zones and we have no choice but to explore them" (p.156). The vision of a new dawn breathes the promise of spiritual fulfillment into Brossard's entire corpus.

She has always known that work on language is the key not only to creative expression, but also to philosophical/theoretical work, and to the transformation of cultural values and practices. Language produces the ideas, with all their inherent ideological assumptions, of what is collectively taken to be reality. In 1975 Brossard undertook two major initiatives which reveal the central importance she attaches to the relationship between women and language. She organized the first of many special feminist issues of *La Barre du jour:* "femme et langage." She asked all the women who contributed to this issue to address the following question: "How can the woman who uses words daily (actress, journalist, writer, teacher) use a language which, right from the start, being phallocratic, works against her?"[2] In her introductory text Brossard emphasizes the urgency of this question and indicates how pleased she is to discover that this question is also a serious concern for many other women. Her own contribution to this special issue on women and language, "*E muet mutant*" (the mutation of the mute *E*), reflects the radical and aggressive stance she has sustained for almost fifteen years in response to this fundamental problem.

Also in 1975, Brossard gave the opening paper at the annual international conference of writers organized by the Quebec journal *Liberté*, the theme of which was "La Femme et l'écriture." Here again, Brossard insists on the urgency of the problematic relationship between women and language. She stresses simply and very strongly how important it is that women write:

For me, what is important at the present time is that women write, aware that their difference must be explored in the knowledge of themselves who have become subjects, and further, subjects involved in a struggle. To explore this difference is necessarily to inscribe it in a language which questions the sexism of the tongues we speak and write. By that very fact we inaugurate new places for writing and reading; by that very fact we inscribe in culture a literature of the unspoken. An unauthorized and unspoken literature.[3]

Since 1975 Brossard has published more than a dozen significant works of prose and poetry, co-produced the film *Some American Feminists* and played a major role in the collaborative dramatic production *La Nef des sorcières*. In this rich and varied body of work, she has focused centrally on both the magic of words and the inseparability of language and ideology. The astonishing beauty of her creative expression is enhanced for the reader by hearing the ardent voice of a lucid woman moving in a space on which she is imposing her *own* coherence. It makes all the difference!

Throughout this busy period of creative writing, Brossard has also actively pursued her theoretical analysis. Indeed, since theory and poetry are inseparable for her, it could not be otherwise. In addition to her collection of theoretical texts, *Double Impression. Poèmes et textes 1967-1984* (1984), Brossard has also written other theoretical texts, most unpublished, many written while working actively with other women on a specific topic, frequently for a conference. These texts are more intimately related to the realms of the imagination and memory, which she explores with delight when writing her poetry and fiction. It is these texts which she published in *La Lettre aérienne* in 1986.

The Aerial Letter is a collection of twelve theoretical texts arranged in chronological order, the itinerary of analysis and theoretical reflection followed by Brossard between 1975 and 1985. They speak of her "desire and will to understand patriarchal reality and how it works ... for its tragic consequences in the lives of women, in the life of the spirit" (p. 35). Each theoretical text is followed by a carefully chosen passage from the work of poetry or fiction she was writing at the time. The theoretical text illuminates the entire creative work, while the creative work, which still continues on its independent career, is actually what makes the spirit of the theory manifest.

Reflections on language, abstract thought, vital emotion and compelling vision are all integral components of Brossard's writing process. She uses "a sensual and cerebral capacity which lends itself to a form of original concentration" (pp. 85-86). She goes beyond seeming paradox to reintegrate in the human spirit the various intellectual activities that dominant cultural traditions have fragmented: "a previously unheard-of knowledge (intellectually speaking), unfurls from

13

this. It presupposes a form of contemplation and concentration for the woman who writes, that I call the thought of emotion and the emotion of thought" (p. 76). Her holistic approach, the inseparable conjunction of emotion, thought and sensation in her work, offers theory with a radical difference. Her starting point is the subjectivity of women as the site of difference: "... they cannot write if they camouflage the essential, that is, that they are women" (p. 73). Brossard was one of the first to recognize the importance of writing from such a perspective: "Ecrire: je suis une femme est plein de conséquences."[4]

This difference, on which Brossard insists, is an appproach to intellectual activity which recognizes the determining role played by the individual as conscious subject in a "certain body."[5] This approach considers ideas and concepts as inseparable from imagination and is rooted always in the material reality of the world as known by sensation and experience, and never in logic alone. This leads Brossard to expose many unspoken assumptions as pure delusion and to refuse to recognize any ideas which lay claim to belief by virtue of universal and transcendant validity. Brossard has known this with passion throughout her writing career. For her, human experience and its meaning find their source in each individual:

One has the imagination of one's century, one's culture, one's generation, one's particular social class, one's decade, and the imagination of what one reads, but above all one has the imagination of one's body and of the sex which inhabits it. (p. 82)

The history of patriarchy shows us all too well the way in which presumably eternal truths and disembodied ideas lend themselves to the violent abuse of power.[6]

In dominant patriarchal culture, only experts *know*. Women do not *know*, nor do they possess knowledge, for knowledge is power, particularly when knowledge establishes continuous links between the past and the present. When women recognize the arbitrary nature of these ideas and the contingent status of the discourses which support them, the consequences will likely be so radical as to bring about a mutation of the human species.

Brossard captures the essence of this radical shift in the first text of *The Aerial Letter*, "Turning-Platform," by using the incomplete fragment: "If I know ecstasy" (p. 40). When the narrative voice of the written text speaks in the first person, speaks in the feminine without reference to the male, and affirms her own active, desiring subjectivity, revolutionary transformation of the institutions of society and its cultural practices will follow. What will the future hold? How will the fragment – "If I know ecstacy ..." – be completed? What if several such fragments / women-in-action, all starting their quest by proclaiming "If I know ecstacy," whirl in the same conceptual space? There is a collective memory to reclaim, an imaginary realm to explore, bodies of culture to form. How exciting it is to ask what will happen if we know ecstacy.

The theoretical texts of Brossard are not detached intellectual exercises seeking to reveal unchanging truths. They claim no authoritative status. They assume the relativity of having been written in the fullness of personal experience. They call out to the fullness of other lucid subjects. They insist on the central importance of sensation, pleasure, anger and desire felt intensely and immediately. To her theoretical reflections Brossard brings emotional and sensuous vibrancy, ardent vision, delight in play, joy in celebration, and vigour for untrammelled exploration. Brossard displays no fear of seeing what happens when women and the texts of women are recognized as the site of ecstacy, anger, rupture, displacement or dissonance. She sees the undertaking as an initiation rite. It is an adventure for which models and codes do not exist in any literature.

"What is an *aerial letter?*" While the two words used by Brossard in the title of this collection are both familiar, the concept they refer to is not something you can pin down with certainty. This "letter" is sent to communicate information and convey a message. Like an "airmail letter," *The Aerial Letter's* message must reach its destination as quickly as possible with speed, intensity and direction. And yet, because the familiar expression is slightly altered in the title, we are inclined to stop and think about the meaning of each word. It seems that Brossard has chosen this suggestive but ambiguous title to emphasize right from the start that it is important to think about the sense of words, their materiality and their production of meaning. Their rich connotative power can be invoked to enflame the imagination to the point of ecstacy. It can also, and too often, be invoked to deceive and oppress. In the case of the title of *The Aerial Letter,* Brossard wants the reader to think about the sense of each of the two words separately. As soon as we do, we have a preview of the book's language, questions, images and themes.

The adjective "aerial" suggests associations on many levels of meaning: air, light, space, movement (in three dimensions, and particularly elevation through flight and soaring), freedom, vertigo, breath, spirit, sight and vision, eye and gaze, lucidity, communication, music. The noun "letter" is equally suggestive. As I have already mentioned, letters we send allow us to stay in touch with one another. As Jovette Marchessault stresses, letters are waves of energy which give birth to women's culture and spread its traditions. Letters also form the alphabet. The word "letter" calls forth associations with words, speech, writing, expression, communication, meaning, creation, stories and history, thought, imagination, discourse, literature, knowledge, culture, laws and social institutions. The letter opens the door into the affairs and politics of human society.

There is considerable play in this book with the notion of "roots," roots which are, if we are talking about plants, "what grows in the opposite direction from the stalk," and also, if we are talking of language, the "irreducible element of a word, obtained by the elimination of all *inflections* and *grammatical markers* and which constitutes a *base for meaning*" (p. 105). Roots unseen and unnoticed, though nonetheless vital as the original, nourishing part of plants or words, serve well as an image for the situation of women in patriarchal culture. This situation must be reversed so that roots, without being ripped from their essential environment, are brought to the light. Brossard's texts are a persistent return to the roots of words and things, to the origins of women in order to rid social organisms of their "inflections" and to reveal what serves in culture as a "base for meaning." Brossard also makes use of a second word evoking the image of "roots." That word is "radical," a word which we use most often now with political connotations. It is "urban *radicals* of writing in movement" (p. 80) who, by initiating themselves to one another, achieve sufficient intensity to go back to their roots, to vital sources, and bring about this necessary reversal.

As a result, the "root," hidden in the unchanging and unnoticed territory assigned by patriarchy culture to women, is, by a seeming paradox, transformed. In celebration, Brossard's text, "From *Radical* to Integral," proclaims that the *root* has become *aerial*:

> *Now with intensity, will I root myself in the place that resembles me. Now with intensity will I initiate myself to other women. The roots are aerial. The light which nourishes them, nourishes, at the same time, the tender shoots (the culture) and the root. The root is integral and aerial, the light coherent.* (p. 106)

17

As Brossard states in her introduction, language constitutes the main subject of *The Aerial Letter.* Language is something quite other than a simple medium of communication, even though this is what people generally think language is all about. For this reason, it might be helpful to consider some of the concepts about language with which Brossard works.

Because it is a system of signs / symbols, language is transcendence. It makes it possible to reflect upon the material world, to see order in what may not originally have order, to detach oneself and establish distance between the conscious subject and the outside world. It is because language works on this principle of *abstraction* that it is possible to form notions of meaning, ideas of truth and reality, systems of value. On the basis of language, all collectivities which see themselves as having a common culture derive an equally common system for the representation of the material world and human experience in it, as well as a common symbolic order, common myths. The individuals who are members of the collectivity sense that they inhabit the same context, common notions of space, time, value: a coherent ontological landscape.

This relationship between the material and the conceptual, between the immanent and the transcendent, is vital for the emergence and perpetuation of human culture. And it is in this relationship that language plays the operative role, authoritative texts serving to consolidate and confirm collective consensus regarding meaning and value. The ideology behind dominant discourse will determine what is perceived as interesting, which expressions are legitimate, what will be retained to function as historical object, what experience is to be legitimized on an ontological basis. Accompanying language in its role of representing the forms of reality is the eye and its gaze, the gaze too often used to establish a logic which opposes the seeing subject and the external object, an object which is alien and must be dominated. When transcendence and abstraction occur, producing meaning, knowledge, notions of reality – the basis for culture – the product is never value neutral. The conventions at work determining the way the elements and structures of language are used are a function of the material situation and the ideologies of the dominant group exercising power within the collectivity. The activities, experiences, desires, fears and fantasies of that group are reflected in language conventions. Seeing their reflection reproduced everywhere around us, because our education has conditioned us for them, they seem natural and a matter of common sense. They may even seem to have a pre-ordained status of truth. That is their danger:

> Reality is a familiar idea which appears obvious. Reality absolves one from one's consciousness; it is our "clear conscience" which justifies our daily acts. At the very beginning of our lives, reality is the part we learn by heart: it is the metonymy which takes the place of memory, vision, and sense. Women's reality is not men's reality. (p. 149)

In effect, since men have exercised effective control in our society for thousands of years, our language is patriarchal and sexist in its basic structures, and so are the generally accepted notions of what is real. Brossard calls dominant notions of truth and reality "opaque semantic reality" (p. 146). All that is excluded from such a construct is cast into non-reality, non-sense, non-existence. The normal practice of language then stands as an implacable barrier to all women in their writing and in their very relationship with the world. To illustrate such alienation in a striking way, Brossard raises the question whether, in their relationship with culture, women can identify with the great Ulysses and his heroic quest, or whether our origins lie buried with the Sirens whom Ulysses feared as dangerous temptresses drawing him to his death (p. 41). The

19

male-dominated traditions of Western civilization, with their emphasis on the Word, go back at least as far as Socrates, Plato, Aristotle and the biblical fathers. They have been enshrined in legal, judicial and poetic codes. They continue to function all too well in the languages of today's educational systems, of the mass media and in the jargon and canons of the professions. The philosophical foundation and value system on which this patriarchal culture rests have produced notions of reality, common sense, evidence and scientific proof which exclude women from the realm of knowledge and deny their experience. They replace women's perception of what is real with fictions and myths arising from the way men in positions of power need to see the Other – women and all groups they presume to dominate: "The image of woman is a foreign body in the eye of man" (p. 125).

Brossard has chosen to work on the signifying process of language to reveal its arbitrary and biased nature and to transgress its conventions: "that stony urge to start over again" (p. 125). This is not an easy task, for its origins are deep indeed. There is a concrete need to situate oneself in the terrain of one's own imaginary and so to have the vision and energy to "trans / form," to produce shifts in meaning, slippage or "semantic divergence," to "take on reality," to see the world otherwise and so, like Alice, to pass through the looking glass rather than being caught in the conventional reflection it offers (pp. 98, 106, 68).

Since language, along with the codes and systems it generates, is by nature a collective institution, Brossard cannot work alone: "To be here and now a conscious woman and without solidarity, that makes no sense" (p. 46). Her project of using language to express difference and so to establish a fresh structural and ideological basis for culture is necessarily undertaken in company with those who can also see beyond the deceptive "realities" and "truths" of patriarchy: feminist writers and readers who offer the promise of "critical appreciation" by forming an interpretative community which rejects the official canon of definitive texts, and women writers of the past whose voices remained unheard but whose books can now be opened and understood. "How then *to make collective sense?*":

> if patriarchy can take what exists and make it not, surely we can take what exists and make it be. But for this we have to want her in our own words, this very real integral woman we are, this idea of us, which like a vital certitude, would be our natural inclination to give sense to what we are. (p. 103)

With these women, Brossard proposes to inscribe through writing all that she knows to be real in the experiences of women.

In the work of Nicole Brossard the women who are capable of radical displacement, the "resolute ecstatic women" (p. 40), are Amazons and urban radical lesbians, they being the only women not "man-made," (p. 141) not invented by Man:

> Lesbians are the *poets* of the humanity of women and this humanity is the only one which can give to our collectivity a sense of what's real.
>
> The lesbian is a threatening reality for *reality*. She is the impossible reality realized which reincarnates all fiction, chanting and enchanting what we are or would like to be. (p. 121)

While remaining at the political centre of human affairs, urban radical lesbians are in such completely different conceptual space they can toss out paradigms which do not make sense for them. They open themselves up to new dimensions of space ("*ma* continent" p. 123), and of time, both personal and collective ("memory made plural, multifaceted mirrors";

"remembering forward into the open" p. 81; 44). In order to convey this idea of dis-placement, Brossard frequently uses the image of a void or a gap as a necessary break in the continuity of patriarchal culture:

> Producing a void, a mental space which, little by little, will become invested with our subjectivities, thus constituting an imaginary territory, where our energies will begin to be able to take form. (p. 111)

> To write, for a lesbian, is to learn how to take down the patriarchal posters in her room. It means learning how to live with bare walls for a while. It means learning how not to be afraid of the ghosts which assume the colour of the bare wall. (p. 135)

Such a radical break, which relies on women's strong and sustained solidarity, will produce a new cultural context on whose screen a strong and real image of women can be projected. This fresh and dynamic imagination of women will bring with it a new imagination of the world's reality as well.

When patriarchy determines the symbolic order whereby society and its culture are directed, women, excluded from transcendence, and dominated because they comprise the central component of all that is immanent, remain objects in the field of male desire. If the dawn of new paradigms is to occur, in whose light women's subjectivity can function, we must literally give birth to ourselves, bring ourselves into the world using letters and ideas arising from abstractions which suit us: "a symbol sparks recognition, ... becomes a *captivating image*" (p. 126).

To give focus to such a goal, we need the vision of a utopia. Brossard imagines and creates such a utopia in the hologram, her three-dimensional and integral woman:

(in my universe, utopia would be a fiction out of which
would be born the generic body of she who thinks) ... I
would have in my mind only the idea that she could be the
one through whom anything can happen. I would have
her to imagine while writing her an abstract woman who
would slip herself into my text, bearing fiction from so far
that from afar, this woman with the properties of words,
she would have to be seen coming. Infinitely virtual, for-
mal in every dimension of knowledge, of method and of
memory. (p. 147)

Women sharing the vision of such a utopia make words
change their meaning. This dream and quest allows us to
make such change reality.

This brings me back to my earlier remarks about Brossard's
writing that ideas never exist in detached isolation. They are
always situated in a material context. This is equally true of the
vertiginous image of the three-dimensional, integral woman,
who takes form only in the text. In order to become a reality
present in the public forum, transforming the reality which
currently holds a monopoly there, this integral woman must
be written:

... writing is memory, power of presence, and proposition.... in writing I become *everything*.... In writing, I can
foil all the laws of nature and I can transgress all rules,
including those of grammar. I know that to write is to
bring oneself into being; it is *like* determining what exists
and what does not, it is *like* determining reality. (p. 139)

Working on language, in effect working language as the
sculptor works her clay, brings both understanding and the
necessary skill to play with letters differently. If we are to get
out of the closed circle created by vicious and violent cultural
practice, we must take a good look at the way in which words

and structures of language *make sense*. We must speak in our own voice – asking our own questions, giving form to those sensations we know and value, weaving networks which mirror our own patterns, writing and reading texts which allow us to see our experience in an integral and luminous way – in order to *make sense* in the dynamic way which serves our own imaginative, creative, intellectual and political purposes. *The Aerial Letter* is an exciting example of how this can be done, of how many vistas remain for us to explore. On the wings of the letter, we can pass through the looking glass to a fresh and dazzling symbolic order where the air we breathe and we drift on reveals tremendous sources of energy which, when we get in touch with them, move our entire being to ecstasy and into a new reality.

The "aerial letter" of this book is the missive of an urban cultural militant. Her radical revolt has led her to open space for herself alone and with other women in revolt, to engage in combat, to know great anger, to discover wonderful enthusiasm. She envisions utopias, while knowing the struggle and the journey can take place only in the all-too-distressing streets of the city. Hers is an initiatory quest which takes her on a voyage in unaccustomed dimensions. She moves and writes with the ardour of the stimulated and aroused female body. She undertakes her quest, and participates in the "conquest," with words as her weapon, words used as patriarchal culture has never imagined.

The source of the letter's energy is found in the synthesis of strong emotion and compelling thought – the emotion of thought, the thought of emotion. Brossard denounces the lies that enslave; she exposes the ways in which language has been perverted to serve the abuse of power; she plays with letters and words in order to free them and those who use them for vital creative expression; she fills the mind and the body – the space of spirit, imagination, sensation and desire, the space of concept, image and myth – with vertigo, the dizzying perhaps terrifying vision of new orders which also evoke strange echoes of old knowledge.

Louise H. Forsyth

NOTES

1. Letters ... are like a pulsation which is born and spreads itself out in continuity of the literary tradition of women's culture. (Except for passages drawn from *The Aerial Letter*, translated by Marlene Wildeman, all translations in this introduction are my own.) References to *The Aerial Letter* will be included in this text parenthetically.

2. "Comment la femme qui utilise quotidiennement les mots (comédienne, journaliste, écrivain, professeur) peut-elle utiliser un langage qui, phallocratique, joue au départ contre elle?" *La Barre du jour*, 50 (Winter, 1975), p. 8-9. Nicole Brossard co-founded *La Barre du jour* in 1965.

3. "Pour moi, ce qui est important actuellement, c'est que des femmes écrivent, conscientes que leur différence doit s'explorer dans la connaissance d'elles devenues sujets, et plus encore sujets en lutte. Explorer cette différence, c'est nécessairement l'inscrire dans un langage qui questionne le sexisme des langues que nous parlons et écrivons. C'est par le fait même, amorcer des lieux nouveaux d'écriture et de lecture, c'est par le fait même, inscrire une littérature de l'inédit. Interdite et inédite," "La Femme et l'écriture," *Liberté*, 106-107 (July-October, 1976), p. 13.

4. "To write: I am a woman is full of consequences," *L'Amèr, ou le chapitre effrité* (1977), p. 43.

5. As is evident in *The Aerial Letter*, the concept of the "certain body," proposed by French writer Roland Barthes, appeals to Brossard (see "Coincidence"). It means simply that human beings can never achieve the state of pure thought. They are always in a physical body, in the material world, and in the flow of historical time. Their thought is

always, therefore, a function of their material condition. Patriarchy offers the example of many ideologues who would like us to forget such limitation and relativity of ideas so that they might claim the power to make their notions prevail universally.

6. For Brossard's description of "patriarchy at full gallop in our lives" (p. 59), exercising its monopoly by virtue of its having seized absolute control over society's conceptual space, imposing its truth as "*the* Truth," see "Access to Writing: Rites of Language":

> Let's imagine that this masculine plural, better known as Man, takes up, in all its splendour, all its mediocrity, with all its fears and ecstasies, the entire field of semantics and the imaginary. Let's imagine that in all its glorious pride, this masculine plural "I" has effectively taken up all significant space in the order he himself has conceived. Let's imagine the worst, that in one fell swoop of spirit and pen, he has crossed out Woman's existence, decreed the inferiority of females, and invented THE woman. (p. 139)

Translator's
Introduction

When I began translating this book, I found myself in a very privileged position with a specific task at hand and clear feminist obligations: translate Nicole Brossard's *La Lettre aérienne* for English feminist readers, and, in the process, create a certain English lesbian feminist perspective on Nicole Brossard, writer and literary theorist, as she "masters working the horizon" of women's culture. However, from the outset, the "specific" task proved to be constantly challenged by various practical and ethical questions, and, with every attempt to address them, the "certain" English lesbian feminist perspective was transformed.

To begin with, there was the question of who I was translating for. I told myself that feminist literary academics would be able to read *La Lettre aérienne* in French, so that clearly I was not translating primarily for them. If my translation were based on a desire to make Quebec feminist literary theory more accessible to English-speaking Canadian feminists (and it was), could this mean I would be flying a letter of international stature to regional airports only? But if I were to build it to meet American standards so that, at a glance, women around the world could identify it as (North) American, would I not be contributing to a growing tendency to gloss the differences between Canadians and Americans, a trend many of us recognize as having deleterious effects on Canadian culture? Furthermore, if I were to produce a translation that bore no identifiable marks of its Canadian origins, would I not be reneging on the more fundamental of Brossard's theories on why women write? Or translate? Then, finally, as a Canadian feminist writer and translator, what were my translation responsibilities with respect to Quebecois literary culture "in the feminine?"

On the one hand then, there were questions related to the nature of Brossard's voice in translation, which is, in fact, my voice representing hers, and on the other hand, technical concerns regarding the transmission of feminist strategies developed in French by Brossard and other feminist writers.

Ultimately, the translation of French feminist strategies proved to be a matter of concrete analysis and decision-making. I found that the genderlessness of English often robbed the French text of its feminist strategies, and in the case of *essentielle*, I simply adopted the French word. The English language has been borrowing words throughout the centuries; the difference here is that we are choosing what to borrow. We are consciously speeding up the development of feminist culture, which in turn cultivates politically conscious female culture. (I would have gladly borrowed French *jouissance* and its verb *jouir,* if I had thought we anglophones could learn to take pleasure in these words, but instead I settled for "ecstasy" as a rare, and reserved, but probable English equivalent.) Other instances required that the word "woman" be added in the English text, whereas in French a feminist use of the *–e* inflection indicates the subject is female. But how to recreate in translation the inexpressible joy that races through a woman's heart when, in the course of her reading, she sees that the grammatical structures keeping women "outside the magic of words," for as long as can be remembered in the history of womankind, have now been turned to women's advantage? The ecstasy of the text. How to accomplish this in English, where the change must take place primarily in syntax?

With these questions to contend with, you may wonder how I ever got started. The truth is that from the moment Maureen FitzGerald, managing editor at The Women's Press, asked me if I would like to translate *La Lettre aérienne,* I was

off like a long-distance runner, with hardly a moment's introspection as to whether I could afford to consecrate the time
such a project would involve, or whether, when the time came
for lift-off, I would be able to get this (collected) aerial vision
off the ground. *La Lettre aérienne* was only a few days' old at
that point, but already it had got "under my skin." I also knew
La Lettre in translation would have enormous impact on lesbian and feminist writers, and I felt honoured to have been
asked to deliver it.

I worked through the questions of register and intention as
they came up in process, always balancing my ethical obligations to the author with what I considered the essential *Letter*
to be transmitted, both as a specific book and as a collection of
texts bringing liberty to all women. I struggled against my
impulse to make the work accessible, for Brossard's work is
not by nature accessible, and the beauty of her thinking is
probably most appropriately appreciated when it appears
abstractly in one's own reflections. But by keeping strictly to
the post-structuralist "code," was I not catering more to the
academic feminists and possibly abandoning the reader who
had wanted to know about Nicole Brossard's theory but who
couldn't read her in French? – and now, not in English either?
My solution was to keep the code words but to enrich the text
in which they were rooted. In one very significant instance,
"une écriture de dérive," I could neither keep the code word
(as I had been able to do with "combat," for instance) nor provide a direct translation into a single English word. My solution was an interweaving of "writing adrift," "writing that
deviates from the sense one would have expected the text to
take," and "elusive derived writing."

There were, however, other translation dilemmas which
posed ethical questions of another sort. For instance, when is
it appropriate to create in English a literary device which mirrors the form and intention of the source text but not its actual
words, given that the actual words do not find a suitable

counterpart in English? Is the translator ever forgiven for having temporarily abandoned the sustaining metaphor of a given fragment in the interests of continuity in the target language? And what does one make of a fecund textual situation in the target language when it is the natural correspondent to a relatively straight-forward passage in the source text? Is this unexpected richesse actually a long-term complement to an original predication for which earlier the English language had barely been adequate? Does the translator curtail her impulse, deny her intuition, and reproduce faithfully the passage where abundance in English would appear unwarranted? Or does she take it as a gift, and make of it the bloom which earlier failed to blossom? Does the source text narrowly interpreted get carried along in the translator's subconscious as unfinished business, and, left to its own devices, is it then set down eventually in the target language? To be sure, these are questions of literary ethics, and perhaps questions of lesbian feminist literary translation meta-ethics. It has not been my intention to provide answers to these questions here. Rather, I wanted to air some of the issues involved, in the interests of furthering awareness of the political and ethical stance available to the translator in the contemporary practice of the art of translation.

◊

I wish to thank Nicole Brossard for her cooperation, her unfailing enthusiasm for my work, and her willingness to believe in my solutions. I would also like to express my gratitude to Lisette Girouard, my lover and literary team-mate, whose dedication to this project went far beyond the grounds of loverly and literary obligation. I would like to thank the two feminist publishing houses involved, Les Editions du remue-ménage and The Women's Press, for being there in the first place, and for capably providing the practical and supportive means to carry out this lesbian feminist dream. I thank Wendy Waring for her perceptive, generous, and spirited editorial assistance. I thank Rona Moreau for her extremely competent hand at the controls, and I would also like to thank DiDi Khayatt and Linda Stowell, who acted as outside readers of my initial efforts, Jeffner Allen for permission to use her expression "remembering forward into the open" and Lou Nelson for the concept of "writing that eludes." In the interests of wholeness and continuity, and at the request of Nicole Brossard, all translations appearing in this book are my own.

Marlene Wildeman

To Julie

PREFACE

I believe there's only one explanation for all of these texts: my desire and my will to understand patriarchal reality and how it works, not for its own sake, but for its tragic consequences in the lives of women, in the life of the spirit. Ten years of anger, revolt, certitude, and conviction are in *The Aerial Letter*; ten years of fighting against that screen which stands in the way of women's energy, identity, and creativity. Ten years of curves, graffiti, erasures, and writing, in order to exorcise that "curse."[1] I had to "come to grips with words," in order that, from the heated emotional struggle, the three-dimensional women who nourish my desire and my hope would spiral forth.

The Aerial Letter includes texts such as "Turning-Platform," which transcribes the discomfort of trying to overthrow patriarchal law from within, and the void into which we are thrown when we try to extricate ourselves to any degree. A void of despoiled meaning. Other texts demonstrate my frank enthusiasm, while still others, such as "The Aerial Letter," yield textured landscape, where the intersection of ideas and images produces a kind of exploratory relief.

Here everything is predisposed to writing and language, all of it working to undo "woman," that enigma so harmful to us: a male-core fiction, its form inscribed in the masculine.

Addressed to writing, *The Aerial Letter* is a question put to both the heart of everyday reality and the utopian sequences

---

1. Quotation marks, when obviously not a direct quotation, will be indicative of Brossard's emphasis. Single quotation marks indicate the translator's emphasis.

35

which traverse our thoughts, words, and deeds. I like to think of the Letter as that "critical" space where we are learning to see the nature of our desires, in slow motion and on fast-forward; in fine detail, and brought together as a whole.

I don't know whether, with time, memory inclines us to go over in detail the faces of those with whom we worked in a movement in collective enthusiasm, but I would like to thank all those women who, in one way or another, as activists, writers, filmmakers, barmaids, publishers, animators, musicians, translators, actors, journalists, booksellers, photographers, and critics, and all those given to dance the night away, have taught me to recognize the multiple sound of voices which, in us, speak radical.

N.B.

TURNING-PLATFORM

FOR ONCE I WANT to speak neither of nor for other people. I want to take a tour of myself on the turning-platform. Mine: visceral, cerebral, chemical. Forgetting nothing of a history which is beginning to teeter in the post-survival era, that is, outside its own reach.

For the rest of my days I'll be a spinning top, a relentless spiral, stuck fast in the spew of those last words the phallo-cracy will address to the new values settling in. I am thus in history until the end of my days; and whatever the unformu-lated certitudes or affirmed theoretics I manage to maintain about the procedures for transformation and mutation of the species, I'll have to be in the fray. Rudely accosted, I must pro-test. I cry out, I dream, I want things to change. I write, there-fore. I know the content of the text I will write to the very end of my days: the quest of my orgasmic body, the knowledge of my body's ecstasy. This body – covered by laws, interdictions, words – wants to speak (to condemn the law which enforces its repression ... what is obstructed here is desiring, and desire writes, empowered by the very law it transgresses); it wants to know the ecstasy of its own energy.

My woman's being uses men's knowledge to better resist and annihilate the violence and oppression on which this knowledge of men (of humanity) is built. All bodies know their fragility before the beast. The beast is in power. I write so that I won't be his dozing beast of burden. On these last days of my internment, the beast consumes itself.

In the days when I thought like a man, I had simple ideas.

37

Now, I have two sets. My form is encumbered by the I / me who didn't gaze upon my navel enough before it disappeared completely in the ninth month of the birth of the other, girl, her's an obvious umbilicus, like a wound.

My form is encumbered by the refound feminine. I am pregnant with a form I'm not able to make my own and which marks me in my difference and in my other subject. I am made of man's knowledge and of a feminine condition: a hybrid. Patient, due to the luxury of a strength acquired with the help of *ideology's* institutions, not to mention of groups for *ideological struggle* (the circle quickly closed on the little academic who contested for her brothers an inheritance to which she herself would never be entitled); aggravated, for if I long pretended not to remember the little girl, the adolescent, the young bride, today it is I who crop up face to face with an opaque image, I who still do not acquiesce totally to the intimate memory of empty Sundays in white; and if I crop up at all it is by virtue of my alliance with other women, all in the same troubled waters, stretching out our fingers on the turning-platform, history's island, on whose shores from now on we have taken hold. History picks up speed around an empty centre – a white centre – before plunging into its destructive depths. I am part of what accelerates, what points to the last bridges between a reproductive sexuality (our mythic or idealistic modalities are there only as delayed self-realizations, programmed to retard us in longterm sadomasochism) and a bisexuality of a new order of consumption.

Difficult to clearly express reason and knowledge in a language for which the raison d'être is to be maternal. Who serves me when I dine, who pulls the covers up over my fantasy during the night, who is there for me when I cry or rage against powerlessness. Dad, Mum, you haunt me **like two strangers.**[1] As I eat up my living; as I earn my living. *I sit to the*

---

1. The phrase "like two strangers" appears in English in the original. English words in the source text will appear in bold print in translation.

table. My mother is sweet and understands me. One aunt (there's always one in the family who knows absolutely everything) says things I don't understand yet. My father has nothing to say. Other men speak in his place. Here, the fathers keep quiet and the mothers whisper. You have to make an effort to hear what it's all about. Make an effort in order to live and speak normally. Making an effort to be normal, that's what it is to be colonized.

I exert myself elsewhere of course, to write. To help the body get by. To cut a path through the trickery, the obvious, the effects of conditioning. To know the explorian female body, so knowledgeable from myriad cells, memory, and fiction in the cortex.

I'm tired of having a body of compartmentalized parts, a 'corps-capital,' a body whose stories are told by intermediaries. The troubling text is no doubt composed of the history of this fatigue, spread out live in the ghetto of the arts, where the powers that be – lacking imagination – go looking to scare something up (as they would in a brothel, a harem, a "hole") something with which to revive their potency.

I have a score to settle with Knowledge[†] because it terrorizes me from the moment it forces me to school, that is, forces me to learn more about the master's fantasies than about knowledge itself. And all this takes a very long time to sort out. Now I select within knowledge, as though I were in a supermarket. I know the things I want. Unconsciously, and for all time, the knowing body opposes itself to the learned letter. But, everybody knows, what counts is the letter. I write in

---

[†] As a woman and a Québécoise. I have a score to settle also with what's easy (with what would be typical). And I refuse to be typical (symbolic or exemplary) in a scene of alienation under the eye of the master (he alone defines what is typical and what is not), amused by folklore and vitality, fascinated by the gaze he fixes on such beautiful beasts and more beautiful still because so passionate, dishevelled or arrogant, but most certainly resplendent with interesting symptoms. *(Author's note in original French edition.)*

self-defense. If I can find the lost stream, writing interests me. And, of course, it will appear to me like something no one's ever seen before, though it will simply be the continuation of one and the same process: surviving, in spite of my sex, my species, with my reptilian brain, my "thinking cap," and my new cortex.

Typical or different, it amounts to the same thing because, in the end, difference distinguishes between a power and a non-power. Power of words, political power. Power which encompasses differences, appropriates them like an organism which transforms the dimensions of its stomach according to its appetite. The mouth keeping always the same opening.

My own body is my difference and my sole standard for measuring pleasure and pain. I cannot speak us without first knowing how to reply in I. "If I know ecstasy," I am transposed. I have at my disposal a domain of writing and this domain can summon together the us of the *retort* each one of us is; we all have the build for it. It sows doubt. It breaks away, and brings up the question of liberation. It makes imperative a time of historic solidarity. Resolute ecstatic women.

I me it: I can't deprive myself of it. The equilibrium needed in order to survive this non-renunciation is found in the solitary intimate act of writing – the personal of our political ('social' would be too nice) condition – an endless wanting to understand, which spreads out, seeking for itself, for its reading vision, the voluptuous practice of seeing further and further away forever.

(crossing the field of sirens, would this involve pleading or conventional entreaty? But how from writing would she make of herself this verdant within, flowing with foreknowledge, its images immolated one by one on the page?

you infringe upon me in my skin. I must speak then, squeezed like an enigmatic orange. Queerly dressed in my interests, I watch over them with a carnal and historic necessity. I've had it up to here. The humidity. History beseeches us. For the final heartbreak. The final assault.

the erasure inscribed on my eyeball. Ready to leap. No fixed address, undomesticated. What's your name? Nicole Brossard. What does your father do? He's an accountant. Surname, first name, profession. Brossard, Nicole, writer. How's your mother?)

I write fragment because passing or instantaneous in the continuum.

We women have been made to reproduce (and been had) more than loved whereas we have loved unconditionally and that makes for us a pretty condition indeed. Fine kettle: unspeakable, this circuit, where it is frustrated and exiled from within, where in pure waste of energy it turns in circles; and languishes in madness, disgust, death, which serve the handsome writer to compose, outlawed, his masterpiece and his major works. I do not accept that there are losers and yet, to sense the other or oneself almost fail, that's where the pleasure lies, in the falling away, in the cultural undoing or slip. "If I know ecstasy," there is a sexual loss, an area of abolished reproduction which certainly leaves no trace, nothing, no writing. "If I know ecstasy," this is the fragment, writing the conditional have, inscribing greed, the me who searches in the pantry (not the medicine cabinet) for the ecstatic totality of all these desiring fragments. Euphoriture.

I want us in a single movement which would be this or of the instant, all at once. Am I in the process of writing to the loving one or of signing myself with a force that extends me further and gets lost in words?

My relationship to writing is of the same order as I want you and keep the distance for me between what languishes on our skin, pearls in sweat, and what gets lost elsewhere when later I rise. Gravitate.

I wrote in a common-law relationship with and while men were reading me. But, deep down, I write only under a woman's gaze, feverishly received. Between us, the descent. Restless before the void, which is full to the bottom with sonorous rhythmic breathing. It instructs me, replenishes me, gives me order, and undoes me. This is my most plausible continuity, demanding and ecstatic, my time full when it jumbles the cultural tracks for me, writing to survive someone else's madness, the same and other place of that which is not text but its surface. The ice slide. Snow and scarf and she who hangs onto my neck, who warms me. The blue mist of courtly winter and inside, silk, endlessly surprised. On this occasion, branching out like a translator's version, her slant justifiably oblique.

I see that when I write, I do it in struggle and for my survival. See very well what in my gaze sends me alarmed toward other women and solidarity. No hidden reef: I don't want to have to possess anything or anyone, text or persons, unless it's by mutual pleasure. This is the deduction one makes, and it goes all the way back to that first number in which he decided to inscribe his cash memory. Money ringing in. Grandfather clock, he calculates the hours and imposes his time and his times on me. He grazes on my new shoots. He shuts up: it doesn't blossom: I write. And choose the direction of my gaze when we read together.

How do I write? with a woman's gaze resting on me. Or with the body inclined toward her. Does this mean that I learn from my fatigue? From my exhaustion with another woman? I am not untouched by these feminine spheres where it trembles everywhere, the guts tremble, and the teeth, muscles swell, and the lips, anger, the unutterable. Expelling from oneself all superficiality, where it is required to smile, be nice, to soothe, keep the other warm for the sake of nothing but the other, the other's pleasure and pain. A woman's gaze, which is to say: she who knows how to read. Illiterates of desire that we are, when women know how to read on the body of the other who is similar, it means they know the rigours, the jarrings, the hysterical border inside which works them over for want of an exit. This spurs me on. If I desire a woman, if a woman desires me, then there is the beginning of writing. The word sets about to well up, to gush forth; it breaks us out of our isolation. We do more than keep each other company. We direct our common project. We exist in another difference, but without the foreignness, without the morbid fascination, in a sort of questioning which would go back over the course of exhaustion resistance has made us familiar with, in order not to give in to the existing order. Faced with a slap, a fondling, or a fuck. I do not submit to a woman's gaze, I reroute it to where it must go in, where it makes me cover all distances, reread at breakneck speed all the fragments of me silenced, pieced together or torn apart. Buried. To bury oneself in someone's skirt is the metaphor for understanding that it is with clitoral ecstasy we touch, a capsizing of the species' historical body. "If I know ecstasy," it's because something in my equilibrium is shaken, something of the role which enrolls me. I invert word order. I pass Adam on his left. I split in two with my smooth navel. And there is my certain page.

"If I" allows for all ramification. For remembering forward into the open and for sequencing. It reminds us that everything is possible in the ardent vagueness. But, at the same time, always intercepted. It is lost and connects up with no reality (I know the depths when it is a question of inscribing on paper a discourse which reads by itself). "If I" is fictive, because I know that to tell of myself such as I am in a given environment, this is fragment: dry ink, wet ink, glistening with expanded meaning. Real I would be the other, the draining out, where I would make myself dizzy in the telling, where there would be no end of saying – I am a woman – I confuse foreignness with difference – I have a scar which cuts my belly in two. Noon, when it wearies of being vertical and the sun turns the eye's pupil clear.

I write because I cannot put aside the urgency of myself being mine known by me and intervening in that which hurts me day after day. So that I won't succumb to madness or delirium. Silenced words / absent words. I write; I weigh my words. I figure into the balance. I sink deep into myself in order to understand. In order to exact the "certain body,"[2] to

---

2. Cf. Roland Barthes, *The Pleasure of the Text,* trans. Richard Miller (New York: Hill and Wang, 1975), pp. 29, 30.

exact autonomy, the chemical or electric voyage. For this body is cornered in its fin de siècle and finished future. Forced into invention for each of its words, its embracing, its desires. To speed up all its processes of mastery and ecstasy. Fantasy.

My relationship to desire is undoubtedly less great since the child who has split all landscapes in two and has me take them with condensation on the lens; the eye myopic. And so my gaze is less inclined to take possession of itself than to restore continuity to colour and form in space and from this, my fiction. From one detail seeing the whole and in the whole catching sight of myself, rather than rushing *straight on* to detail and taking it over for myself: taking it.

Around and with women, words, discourse, take form differently. Because we have nothing to prove to ourselves. Our life-belt is that we first understand the energy within, then the power relationship. It follows from what's called taking pleasure in knowledge, when we have to trace words for and before ourselves to clear the stage of all its characters before eventually disappearing in turn as spectator. No more heros, no more victims to immolate, no more plot. An immense calm. Meanwhile, inside, it is initiated to what was earlier given up.

And out of this my fiction. My connection. I venture to know better (other than in opposition; in process, rather) the different layers in me. I make discoveries through language. Through language I open myself unprotected. A space for breathing, the other for looking. And it crosses over, converges; makes itself fully sufficient for the exploration.

I commit myself to this which is my ruin and which transfers me from horizon to uterus. No pretence of the complex. I content myself with me the stranger who is consequential and not other. I step out of line with a carnal consequence only. According to fear in my belly: it's time now. What's the weather like? How old is your child?

I cannot write if in each of my internal networks and circulating blood there is not this surface on which we swim in the hope of waking to the simultaneous silence of self and tumult. I go all the way to the end of me. To be here and now a conscious woman and without solidarity, that makes no sense. What then is this space that is at once struggle, quest, and work which would be a revelation? Which forces me to grind along in the personal, the disarray and compassion when she opens her mouth and screams – without a nerve in her body – the inadmissible.

Her relationship to writing draws breath in blood rising to the brain (if this sex had not served so much to reproduce in the pink and the sweat, this sex, this serf): this sex surpasses its competence: it is ecstatic. And by this fact, contradicts history at the same moment it takes its place within it. For me, this is the risk taken in writing. Signature and initials on history's turning-platform. We burn in vain around its belt, taking risks like circus bets; while it wears holes in itself, or endures, a live white centre, the woman question around which I write myself. Obstructed question, we relieve it of debris left there by other interpretations.

My relationship to writing and to knowledge, which is also its support, seems to be cauterized. Burned as they are, the few (familial and revolutionary) cells inside me are reproduced through a tradition, and by a bourgeoisie, that, although in Europe might have produced new values for its own use, here has been content with dumping, without batting an eye (and will never keep an eye open), for it's the multinationals already here, and that puts the question of bourgeois values and, correspondingly, of the revolutionary struggle, differently. From serf to consumer. From the revenge of the cradle to feminism. From marriage to homosexuality. It strikes one that somewhere must be written the fantasy which flitted between the sea and freshwater. The break, or what brought it about: science and fiction of intervention.

Now this has nothing to do with sex but with the condition ⬚f⬚ or ⬚m⬚. When we no longer make babies together, the future will be the human condition. I take my fulcrum from that point. I'm in no hurry for them to find themselves in me, to take up residence here. Look elsewhere, within yourselves, in your own chest. And I'll look in mine. The only exile I've known came from my condition and not my body. That's the difference.

What is it with the persistent use of I in this text? How does it differ from the I used in the diary, the intimate journal? *I* censors itself as soon as it writes itself. *I* has meaning only in reality, that is, in the written work. On this side, and beyond, *I* dissolves; it decomposes in an anarchy of forms. Me, that's an */* other thing entirely. It already brings me closer to myself than what I am. But it's an esoteric approach I am afraid to use, the *I* cannot use because then *I* would be extreme and vulnerable. "Myself" then is used in fiction in a place which works away at reality, which leads reality to its downfall and explodes all the inexpressible fragments. It is at work here too, but it opens on the inside of elsewhere.

I cannot be sorry for myself alone in this reality. I cannot write entirely alone, but in this reality me in solidarity as in a single body open yes.

In order to rise up. To end this, my scattered-woman cycle, and to take up again at its source what left itself there at the very first spray of white.[3]

But no lost origin. Repressed. Swallowed and defecated. Originally, it multiplies itself in the course of things. Conditions itself. What was lost before I wrote; what is lost when I write? What it reproduces, what I infer from me or my condition?

I speak, by way of the written, to another subject. What is obvious is repressed from speech. To write, that will never be

---

3. Cf. Sartre's "écriture blanche" and Barthes' degree zero, or colourless, writing, meaning writing that is free of any obligation to a preordained state of language.

clear for me. I am overwhelmed, fraught with upheaval. Woman's speech/woman's writing, this is another set of links altogether. The likelihood of which worries me.

Writing it wipes out everything that opposes ecstasy and personal harmony. It wipes out someone, something, somewhere. White writing (?). Another writing, red, damned, condemns forever the part of self burning with rage, the part of the other which burns us slowly, little by little. I pledge myself to going against the grain. I wonder this over and understand its violence. To rise up.

Further exists when I say I want to go further. But I want to stay me because I prefer to learn from myself rather than at others' expense or against myself. Further exists when I write because through it I accomplish desire which is never quite fulfilled; I appropriate myself more by extension than by intention. Shifted forward or back by each fragment written. Up ahead of me. Set back from the essential which wordlessly explores itself, all of a body, all of an all.

Taking risks within, a finger down the throat to make the sleeping muse vomit. To see everything rise up all at the same time; myths burgeon forth, fauna oscillates in the hollows of the chest. She digs. She opens and restores to the glistening walls forgotten images; others are being engraved. The belly is heavy. The waters have begun to spread. Buried even deeper, an elated mother suddenly coincides and begins to get worked up about something. Echo. The crossing over.

"What is learned at the expense of one's body is never forgotten." By the orifices and the surface. By the root. By what circulates in the blood and is later transformed into words. Symbols clinging to the self. A rite of passage toward the exterior where *I* proves itself, submits to the test. And takes up the struggle in order to survive. Bewildered before the mirror, sees condense in its gaze the brimming drop which makes the self run over. Imprints itself on the page. Traces of what loves, gazes, touches.

The approach of text like a scenario of perfect consequences leading to what in itself exceeds. The approach of text, age-old attempt to undo the power which is organized around me, which clasps me firmly in a rape, holds on morbidly until the o in open disappears and until its city is built with so much quick-change artistry that you don't know whether it is looking for a woman or seeking in itself its woman, the malady which has hold of it, and decomposes it. Me, the tender one. Him, obsolete. I don't measure up. I'm too big. I can only exert this power if I shrink, and too much, from fear.

Sketched out in her fantasy, woman does not draw sustenance from herself except in parallel; when she writes, she discovers that one half cannot possibly satisfy her and she looks for a way to pass from the shadow into the clear light of morning – it would be so good for me to rest, me too, after so many nights of bad dreams – it would feel good to stretch myself out on the double bed where I would be sponge and sea without being aware of it, swallowing my words in fantasies where no man, no woman, would come to decree that it's time for me to go to work.

Fury in my eye, I shift. I am displaced by several lines and this recomposes all around me the episode thus begun, thus begun, lets loose, spreads out, enlarging my field of vision, my orbits. What do I risk of exile, if by an ardent breakthrough I make the axon circulate? An excitement. An accomplishment where you, my hysterical one, are surprised to find yourself mobile, traversing the Milky Way, intense, arched by a thousand liaisons, the only woman, page by page, to turn in your cycle. I spend from my gender, from a subject which seeks all subjects, so that a sentence happens, clings onto the hem of a dress, onto the verge of tears. Hangs in the balance.

It may consist of simply filling in all the white squares which made the chess and the check possible. Of crossing spaces no one's crossed before. Abolish conquest. But to write it: play black on white. Cards on the table: I and the ultimate personal of my condition. I within the ice, to make it melt. To feel the leaves starting up. Arouse oneself. Take one's time.

◊

It always brings to light the question of within. Outside, what is obvious is. Within, so that it can speak itself in the fullness of day, become intoxicated with light, the white sun. By day, women chat, by night, they circulate in all the hollow parts of the body, their own, and those which snuggle up against them in sleep. One day, during the day, some women write and at night they sleep so profoundly that they know then how to go deeper without danger. In the morning, they surface and make text of their voyage.

"La plaque tournante," written between March and December 1975, was first published in *La Lettre aérienne.*

An/other woman alone. The difference with her and me is that we know the way upstream, from object to subject. Resemblance, which makes us come together over touch and the idea of us we conceive for ourselves. Us as a function of: formal operation on which we concentrate our energy. Us as a function of, women, can this make sense; can it at least engender movement. Transfixed alive as though we had slipped into the breach we ourselves have created. Immobilized and ardent, at one and the same time. This book, will it be the end product of a fever or is it a major exercise of survival? A pelvic thrust and I am quit of the void. Hands red with ink scratching at the soil above me where patri-girls circulate on dry ground, stretch and put on their face, the one that will match the man's smooth cheek freshly-shaved in the clear morning. Maternal clowns, the king's madwomen. Obliging. I see only their ankles, chained.

The difference is that I cannot live deferred. A stay of transformation, the synthesis of a same singular woman. And it's this same difference I ask of your body, the difference of other woman with my regard. Identical to yours. The same like a differential equation. Derived from our functions. Point-blank in the luminous spectrum. Projected against one another like a polysemic dream.

L'Amèr *ou* Le Chapitre effrité

COINCIDENCE

In male conditioning, male heterosexuality is linked to the male prerogative of a human identity; in female conditioning, female heterosexuality is linked to the denial of that same identity.

The purple september staff

MELTING: I need to find a way to make you understand that I am with you and that my desires are not separate from yours. This thought inspired my body to find the means; later we gave it a name. We called it 'melting.'

Isabel Miller,
quoted by Monique Wittig
and Sande Zeig in
*Brouillon pour un dictionnaire
des amantes*

This body was like extremely reticent to use the usual or, at least, the official body language. It's not homosexuality I have in mind here, though it too seems to have balked at conventional scenes.

Viviane Forrester

It is not by accident that we manage to coincide *women among women*; rather it is the pleasant effect of slowly passing through the initiation leading the body to where rapture is imminent: mobility at the heart of the species, primed in space like an instinctive strategy toward consciousness. Meanwhile, my luminous body has a vivid consciousness of chaos, history, and knowledge, all of them at once, doubly dense.

You can't write *women among themselves* without having to consider the magnitude of this little expression: "do without a man," without hurtling against the writing on the patriarchal wall where all laws that keep us separate from ourselves, that isolate us from other women, are inscribed.

i look at myself and voilà there is present to conquer; I've been daydreaming it all along a tenuous string of words. Circling around the subject, seeking out my spaces. The body, wanting to live, looks for a way to stretch. I don't have to go back to *once upon a time*; I simply look in our saliva for movement, desire's axis, which would have me speak of me, us, now.

this salty air which marks the beginning of transitory palpitations. Little by little, the text begun will begin, tangible. An embrace in the widest part of the liquid flow. I hear, not far away, breathing. It's the times which get confused with time: would I have a past?

i cannot imagine myself confined to vegetation for soon, very quickly, metal, stones, the city, surround me, confine me. This is how spaces have come to be then: from an acute sense of survival. Imperative that we step lively on each front, our muscles agile as a thousand allusions make the circuit of our bellies.

we are the night lights, watchful, highly visible, in the city.

spent the night together. Once in bed we're on our guard, because men are on the prowl all over the neighbourhood and we are – we know this – the *very pulse of their prey*. Space, for us, is a sign of resistance: to keep our distance. Not only to protect each one's vital space, but to make sure daily that the enemy (the one that can seize you at any moment) doesn't come by night as well as day to divert your attention, catch hold of your body, capture thus your proud bearing.

we have never had enough space. And on finding it it's like convergence; you know full well, in the happy posture of hands on hips, a sexual tenderness that covers all urban distance.

where there is space, there are tracks. The still warm tracks of those who have gone before us. Hardly visible these traces, buried, hidden, as we often are, from one another. But traces take up more and more space in our lives. They re-appear as us, come up from out of our childhood, where we were forced to learn the female roles in a vulgar humiliating show before parents and friends.

patience and ardour we must constantly renew in order to make it across the opaque city of the fathers, always on a tight-rope, having to keep our balance, and on all sides, the abyss. For we work without nets.

and everywhere, what meets the eye is only the usual: sex, one's sex, life, childbirth, the 'petites morts'[1] and other circumstances of fictive reality. And one forgets that sex is not this ambiguous representation of the other, that it has sense only in reality, and that this reality in turn has sense only *in the moment,* that is, when reality gets us into *such a state.*

as for desire, it resides only in that space where the cue for the other woman's desire is found. Otherwise, it's something else: 'proxy.'

---

1. A French commonplace for male orgasm.

then there is this obsession held by the overwhelming reality (patriarchy at full gallop in our lives, running after us as if on the last hunt, a final assault on our bodies as women-loving women, lesbians, suddenly forced to react, face to face with reality. The confrontation must take place.

combat:

then, this other reality, from where we begin to exist, and in which girls again find themselves full of intensity, in the process of project, like an essential force circulating among the spaces.

distances: space which in perspective gives the impression of drawing further away. Space which is not a void when I cross it on my fingertips, to be able finally to set down my hand, when your hand with its same identity, offset by the light, comes closer slowly to touch just ahead of me the hand which is transformed cell by cell for the temperature rises and the palm, an echo of late nights, suddenly comes alive for a dance of numbers. Then we can breathe, just at this moment. Distance abolished, we enter into the dense centre of fiction, with which I am obsessed, quite as much as by fictive reality.

whence this other persistent thought, that while cognizant of reality (this does happen to me), I am nonetheless taken with all metaphors enhancing the body. The body perceived like a familiar analogy. All scenarios given sway there: what's never been and – no doubt – what's already very well known, these and other scenarios where one recounts oneself and encounters others civilly in the political figure.

which assures the permanence of desire. And for oneself, fecund necessity as one proceeds. The space between us: allowing our eyes to open slowly in an exercise of precision.

women in search of: seeking perspective in the usage of words come from everywhere to capture our attention, this time, in order to write.

another loving technique: commit an indiscretion with respect to memory, in the water, after remembering a fluent voice close to the ear.

this is how I imagine that one can intercept space so that, above oneself, the body of the other woman is not for one second kept in suspense. Shaken up by all the shams of patriarchy, omnipresent as an automatic slap ... at the moment I write these lines, at the moment where the text is possibly about to begin with a series of expressions such as: the lesbian citizen; watchful women, the night-light lovers; the enchanted lesbian.

and words will then be committed to speaking modalities of anger, humiliation, fear; then the mouth (I know, I am familiar with which foods give the appetite for) will open itself on the enthusiasm for figures which, in the rainstorm, have already changed and change again, day after day, the images of reality.

hole: Languorous holes are made by digging in the sand. Languorous holes are inhabited by one or several women lovers. These are good spots to practice languor, when the sun is hot and you can hear the ocean.

Monique Wittig, Sande Zeig,
*Brouillon pour un dictionnaire
des amantes,*
Grasset, Paris, 1976

HOLE: Symbol of the aperture on the unknown; what opens onto the other side (beyond, in concrete terms) or what opens onto what is hidden (beyond, in terms of what seems apparent) ...

On the imaginary plane, the hole is richer in meaning than the simple void.

Jean Chevalier, Alain Gheerbrandt,
Dictionnaire des symboles,
Robert Laffont/Jupiter, Paris, 1969

void / hole: she says "I am a hole," believing by this, as she's often been informed, that she is of mere nothingness or only this horrible wound that men cannot bear to look at. We know the carnage which ensues.

I say that the text begins here. At the hole, this place that fulfills, overfills me, because it is my *intention*, a happy tension which makes me let go like matter in expansion (and here there is no centre, no axis, and this is in no way chaos). This is the opening (thought, the boundless activity of the body, often comes of it). I say that she who has swallowed, who swallows what comes out of a man's hole, closes herself again with that man's anguish inside her and this is *closure* to all others. Her belly, her arms, her hands, are restless, eager to find the opening once again. In vain, she exhausts herself "in love." And each attempt at fabulated love buries her ever more deeply under her hole, puts her in the hole, causing her, in this way, to lose her opening. But the male lens always sees a hole there, sees first and foremost only a *rap*acious hole there (cf. rape: "this hole begged me for it," says he, before his accomplices on the jury).

I say that by my own energy I know the hole, its texture, its landscape, its rhythm. I am no longer turning in circles in my woman's hole. I acknowledge myself: I am thus capable of knowing. And intervening in the city (the lesbian citizen), with all the other women who acknowledged one another from the moment there was opening.

I am, having gone out through my opening, *of the other side.* Male fantasies and the code they dictate are thus reduced, in my psychological space, to their just proportion, as are those who take their nourishment there. It's crossing the mirror and not the static seduction of it, and I understand this now having another woman before me, that the gaze flickering into life has nothing to do with *setting one's sights.* I do not catch sight of myself in another woman; I cross into a new dimension. And this can't help but affect the number, the wavelengths, the music inside.

"La coïncidence," written in April 1978, was first published in *La Lettre aérienne.*

Analysis: so that for me lips represent a motivation to follow mouths full of affinities. I work here toward dis/integrating the convulsive habit of initiating girls to the male, a contemporary practice of lobotomy. I want in fact to see women's form taking shape in the trajectory of the species.

L'Amèr *ou* Le Chapitre effrité

THE AERIAL LETTER

WE CONCENTRATE AVIDLY ON the processes. Of writing, of desirous being, of ecstasy. We concentrate a great deal on the self. We exert ourselves, and in so doing we summon the other within ourselves to a reality which is transformed. Fiction seeks its own fictional subject and memory alone does not flinch. Memory makes itself plural, essential, like the vertigo that foreshadows an aerial vision. Authentic as a first written draft. With each page, the necessary willingness to start over.

For each time I must enunciate everything, articulate an inexpressible attitude, one that wants to remake reality endlessly, in order not to founder in its fictive version nor be submerged in sociological anecdote.

On the one hand, taking on sociological reality by taking risks within. In order to dissolve its fictive character, in order to foil the impostures of the day-to-day anecdote. Here, a question: the text as I.D. card or identity as a science fiction of self in the practice of creating text? Those who have never been able to speak the reality of their perceptions, those for whom the conquest of personal emotional territory has been precluded politically and patriarchally, will grasp that identity is simultaneously a quest for and conquest of meaning. Desire slowly emanates from what is inadmissible in her project: transformation of the self, and the collectivity. Inadmissible will to change life, to change her life. Imperatives with regard to what in the environment appears intolerable. Identity turns into project when the border between what's tolerable and what's intolerable disintegrates or, one might say, when it no longer holds up. This is when words make themselves void of sense or take on another meaning; take a new turn in the sequence of thought's events. Words begin to turn round on themselves, inciting reflection, inciting thought toward new approaches to reality. And it is also when words begin to oscillate between derision and vitality, becoming, little by little, indispensable strategies for confronting reality's two slopes: the actual and the fictive.

On the other hand, tackling reality the way one takes on a project; so as to take by surprise equations, for they give to the surface of all skin its vitality, its reasoning, if you will. Bathing in the atmosphere of the senses and giving form to enigmas we imagine out of the white, while the certain body[1] refers us back to an implacable geometry: our feverish excitement, a fluidity of text seeking its source. Taking on reality in order that an aerial vision of all realities arises from the body and emotion of thought. Realities which, crossing over each other, form the matrix material of my writing. This text matter, like a fabulous mathematics, relates words to one another. All bodies carry within themselves a project of sensual high technology; writing is its hologram.

I
THE ORDEAL: THE TEST
AND / OR THE PROOF OF MODERNITY

The text, the notion of text, has been, as we well know, subjected in the past few decades to several transformations; most have been a response to the necessity for politico-sexual subversion. The textual site has become the repository for the

---

1. Cf. "le corps certain." Roland Barthes. *The Pleasure of the Text,* trans. Richard Miller (New York: Hill and Wang, 1975), p. 29.

body, sex, the city, and rupture, as well as the theory that it generates, which in turn regenerates text. Text has systematically proliferated, profaning the state of mind of both the petit- and the grand-bourgeois. The ordeal of modernity (Rimbaud's "one absolutely must be modern") as initation w/rite, has been succeeded by "one must be resolutely modern" as political initiation project. The experience of text, understood as crossing through writing, will be transformed by experimentation, that is, by a strategy bound to disrupt.

Everything conspires to ensure that the writing "I" speak desire and not its desire, keeping by this distancing its formal presence, its inherent prestige. In this there is a known principle of seduction whose function is both to excite and to incite. Seduction of what symbolically masters. Thus the textual "I" will say: I will make you neutral, my I, so as to prevent you from letting your origins show, those which might be deemed ideologically suspect, your bourgeois, religious, or feminine origins. I condemn you therefore to anonymity, such that you cannot be co-opted or alienated, like all those little "I's" which capitalism has reduced to marionettes but who, all things considered, can still express themselves – do nothing but, in fact. I intend to, that is, I will speak the "I" which resolutely exists, I choose to speak out, I am subversion, I am transgression. If not, I do not exist. Theoretically.

Just as exposing oneself to everything seemed real to me, the "I impose myself on everyone," which followed in the modern texts of the Sixties, seems to me fictive, like a seduction which has value only by virtue of a convention, a fiction.

It is here that writing begins, that I begin again.

I say that writing begins here between what's real and what's fictive, not between the knowledge we have of one and the intimate experience we have of the other, but between the words that we seek to conceive in their true relationship, so as to get to the bottom of the question, always integral, of thought and emotion; *motifs* and motivation.

We can imagine writing as a *rapprochement,* or as the concrete will to attract toward oneself the essential figures of thought/or even/to see one's desire come *as far as possible,* that is, closer: to the very edge, right to the limits – where it might very well falter. Balance or vertigo, when the "exact expression" illustrates the thought of emotion, when what appears on the page seems like a *coincidence:* a perfect synchronization between explosion and mastery which breaks through to an opening. Each time it must be imagined; what would give *access to.*

I have just said "imagine writing." After all, maybe that is as far as we have come. Forced to drift in total lucidity into the imaginary world of words, tempted by an improbable literature and – since theoretically and ideologically improbable – displacing it toward what we would agree upon calling *fiction.*

But before coming to fiction, I would like to say more about text. I take as a given that the text-fetish, in the sense used by Roland Barthes who wrote, "the text is a fetish object, and this text desires me,"[2] has appropriated Literature, this practice of the written which consists of inscribing, among other things, the expressive part of a memory rooted in an environment at once geographic, social, and cultural, and which recalls the site of our origins as much as it does our first stimuli.

It is in order to avoid that these "unmentionable" origins (ideologically speaking), like those "unmentionables" (sexually speaking), be manifest in one's writing that little by little the writer becomes, according to his own formula, a 'technician' of writing.[3] For the same reasons, the text-fetish will reappropriate Literature (according to the old axiom), this having become prattle, too sentimental, and emotional (a bit

---

2. Ibid, page 27.
3. In the original, "... l'écrivain va devenir selon sa propre formule un écrivant." (p.47)

too feminine, wouldn't you say!). One can at this stage, without answering immediately, inquire whether fiction, or that which I personally would call the fictive text, will in turn appropriate the text-fetish, which now has become too reductive.[4] (In chemistry, a "reducing-agent" is defined as being that which is apt to remove oxygen.)

Let us return once again to text.

To date, we have known a certain experience of text in which there is a vital practice of modernism, and several of these modernist texts are memento-screens testifying to the form emotion and thought have taken over the last thirty years. Emotion which, need I add, in Quebec is distinctly related to urban life. For the city concentrates energy; it calls for *fiction,* ellipsis, and theory, not to mention the politicization of texts. In some, the city stimulates *a modern spirit*; in others, it is responsible for modern *performances.*

I hold that this exciting experience of text which turns about itself, bearing and being borne by its own weight, simultaneously suggests excess, the circle, and the void. I say the circle, for it seems to me that in wanting to break the linearity, it is as if we have been forced into its opposite, to turn full circle, as if the text in this had come to its own end in itself, even were this to explode.

From excess, from the circle (as the sum of fragments accumulated from having been repeatedly shattered), and from the void, I would then translate the results into the feminine by a shift in meaning going from excess to ecstasy, from circle to spiral, and from void to opening, as a solution for continuity.

But I would like to come back to this "impression of void," to which the practice of writing texts lends itself, for it is this *impression* which still motivates some of the lettered few

---

4. In the original, "trop réducteur," 'réducteur' meaning literally 'reducing-agent.'

(professors and critics, among others) to maintain the phobia of the text, an impression of a vacuum they preserve intact, in order to reach the conclusion that research and advances accomplished there are irrelevant.

If in Quebec the literary terrain is changing, this is not a result of criticism but rather because most of the textual few know how to re-read themselves in time. To this, I would add that the writing produced by women in the last ten years has considerably helped textual writers to re-read their work in time. For women have displaced the purpose of writing; the relevance of purpose. This may have been premature for some men, but for women, it came at precisely the right moment.

It is this very "impression of void," I might add, that will disturb and displace the very people who are given to text the way one gives oneself up to the immediacy of pleasure. I have said "impression of void" because the text, we know very well, condenses; it sums itself up in certain words: city, sex, text, body, desire, script, the gaze (that of film, that of photography). The text is an ideogram. In a way, it is because the text condenses (it is not a chatterbox), that it does reduce (it takes the shortest route possible), that it gives this impression of running on empty, or of running wild[5] (something to do with its excessive vitality).

Thus, for those who write text, on the one hand, an improbable Literature (hiding one's roots), and on the other, an impossible text (an impression of void). But the desire to write survives. *Absolutely.*

Lucidity, the yearning for and of text, and for many, their very survival, will exact a new writing: one that drifts, that slips out from under; writing that eludes. Why not then submit proof of imagination by opening a breach: a spiral?

To conclude my remarks about text, one last comment: it

---

5. In the original, "... de faire le vide ou de faire le fou." (p. 49)

was not symbolically important to know who the actual author behind a text was, whether in the flesh, in memory, or in childhood, for text was precisely the formula which permitted the writer not to have to submit to *the test*.

II
THE TEST AS SEEN FROM
THE FEMININE (ENTER FICTION)

Here and now I search in vain for fiction. This fiction, so keenly called for, is in a sense the opposite of utopia for it seeks to compose itself from all that anchors history.

France Théoret

And the Damned of the damned raise themselves up little by little out of imprecision and non-existence.

Jovette Marchessault

Nothing is reassuring for a woman, if not herself, having gone and found herself among other women.

Women write, but at this point in time, they write more than ever with the conscious knowledge that they cannot write if they camouflage the essential, that is, that they are women.

The female body will speak its reality, its images, the censure it has been subjected to, its body filled to bursting. Women are arriving in the public squares of Literature and Text. They are full of memories: anecdotal, mythic, real, and fictional. But above all women are filled with an original all-encompassing memory, a gyn/ecological memory. Rendered in words, its reality brought to the page, it becomes fiction theory.

Faced with text now impossible – because it denies the memory and the identity of its author, because it reduces the body to that of the neuter-masculine – how to, without reverting to a linear literature (that is, narrow and without perspective), how then to render what works at the female body on the inside and all over its surface? How to make use of words when, as Louky Bersianik points out: "The symbolic is the place Man allotted to himself, though this was neither solicited nor called for. In so doing, he usurped the place of the other, that is, that of woman. Then he could say she doesn't exist."[6]

What form could contemporary thought take exactly, giving to words an entirely new flair? For the body has its reasons. How to keep one's distance from words without, for all that, giving up one's place, without ending up neutered and neutralized in one's text, without losing sight of an image of self finally liberated from its negativity, without omitting that which reflects it (women and honour, as Adrienne Rich would say), and that which sense always transforms and extrapolates.

Writing sense / reading sense. A sixth sense is at work in the life of women. Repressed to the point of appearing non-existent, and by this same fact rendered inoperative in the patriarchal system, it seems to me that this sixth sense, for circumstantial reasons in the development of western civilization, is reaching maturity, and that it can, from this point forward, intervene in the reality and even in the fiction that it calls forth or represses. A sixth sense which might bring to mind the transformational role of a "synthesizer" in music, which offers reality from diverse mobile angles, and then orchestrates their differences. A sense which excites / incites the desire to submit proof of imagination and which occasions a spatial shift: the imaginary. A sixth sense which calls into

---

6. Louky Bersianik, *Le Pique-nique sur l'Acropole* (Montreal: Editions VLB, 1979), p. 130.

question the very notion of what we call intelligence; which, taken from its strictest dictionary sense, is "the set of mental functions having as its object conceptual and rational knowledge (as opposed to sensation and intuition)."[7] The limits of this form of intelligence are quickly apprehended. More difficult to grasp is the form of intelligence presupposed by the existence of a sixth sense and the way it works in its role as gatherer of information generated and received by the body. Let us call this a system of perceptions or reality construct.

Women, conditioned not to take their perceptions into account (certain women do, of course, for their own personal stability, at times meeting patriarchal dictature head on), and conditioned never to speak about them, women are bound to see their perceptions as impressions. Through force of circumstance, they will go so far as to have impressions of impressions, to the point where they have the impression that it is all in their head, made up, and that their perceptions are, after all, simply the fruit of their imagination.

This is why we can say, on the one hand, that until now reality has been for most women a fiction, that is, the fruit of an imagination which is not their own and to which they do not *actually* succeed in adapting. Let us name some of those fictions here: the military apparatus, the rise in the price of gold, the evening news, pornography, and so on. The man in power and the man on the street know what it's all about. It's their daily reality, or the 'how' of their self-realization. You know – life!

On the other hand, we can also say that women's reality has been perceived as fiction. Let us name some of those realities here: maternity, rape, prostitution, chronic fatigue, verbal, physical, and mental violence. Newspapers present these as *stories*, not fact.

It is thus at the border between what's real and what's

---

7. My translation, from the *Petit Robert*.

75

fictive, between what it seems possible to say, to write, but which often proves to be, at the moment of writing, unthinkable, and that which seems obvious but appears, at the last second, inexpressible, that this elusive derived writing, writing adrift, begins to make its mark. Desire of/for elusion and desire derived from.

Elusion desire: desire which deviates from the sense one would have expected the text to take – censure with respect to the text's primary intention, at times complete censure: silence.

Desire derived from: desire which originates from an internal certitude and which results therefore in writing that traverses a gynecological memory. Crossing over and crossed through by this memory, one can infer that a woman's writing de-rivets that which is firmly riveted in the patriarchal symbolic order. An approach, and a previously unheard-of knowledge (intellectually speaking), unfurls from this. It presupposes a form of contemplation and concentration for the woman who writes, that I call the thought of emotion and the emotion of thought. A mental space replete with possibilities stemming from a perspective which joyously initiates a shift in meaning. In the text all is moving, like woman's skin on woman's skin, and this occasions a pleasure which lights up intelligence and revitalizes all women who take part.

What is made here in this mental space is History. Without making a scene, biography and daily life are able to circulate so that the *test,* (living/writing) and its deployment (thinking), are transformed.

To write in the feminine then perhaps means that women must work at making their own hope and history, in the one place where these can take shape, where there is *textual matter.*

III
THE AERIAL VISION

A) MEMORY PLURAL

I was moved at the beginning of this text to say: "Fiction seeks its own fictional subject and memory alone does not flinch. Memory makes itself plural, essential, like the vertigo which foreshadows an aerial vision." What should we make of this plural memory which would regale text to the point of transforming it into *fictive text,* that is, a real text, existing before our very eyes but about which we could still have doubts, as if it were unthinkable, even as we *force the spirit to think it,* with exactitude in its form and movement. Think it with the aid of this plural memory which now bathes in, now circulates from one brain to another, cortex and neo-cortex. Think it to the point where the pages, the underlying threads, and the pageantry of the species take on the appearance of live texture.

This body, which the text has fragmented the better to then recompose it as subversive virtue in the contemporary consciousness, this body thought (about) becomes body thinking at the speed of light. A while ago I might have believed it was this body Roland Barthes spoke of, "this body which pursues its own ideas,"[8] but in order to continue writing I need to believe that this thinking body, whose complex texture is made up of infinite individual memories, active and industrious as if madly in love, is still somehow different from that known enraptured body we sometimes manage to touch upon with lines written in a feverish but nonetheless precise hand.

But the body has its reasons, mine, its lesbian skin, its place in a historical context, its particular environment and its politi-

---

8. Ibid, p. 29.

cal content. Under my very eyes, the lines come round on themselves: linearity and shattered fragments of linearity (those ruptures you've heard of) transform themselves into spirals. "Beautiful muscular women in the grass, happy and ferocious, saw their body hair glisten with a thousand scintillae when the memory came to them that surfaces, deep down, gave birth to the consciousness of space (with them)."[9]

My body's plural memory also tells me that "women's memory is torrential when it has to do with torture"[10] – systematic torture which, as Mary Daly shows in *Gyn/ecology,* has been camouflaged in the name of value systems and customs: Chinese foot-binding, the custom of suttee in India, clitoridectomy, gynecology, and contemporary psychiatry. The ravages are extensive. But memory comes back to the surface each time, as though to make a mental synthesis. It is from this synthesis that I take my point of departure; that I start over with each spire of the spiral in order to postulate the meaning of words otherwise – the dictionary has just one of the novel poses struck by these bodies with their memory, skin, cortex, anger, and tenderness.

Little by little, sight replaces the gaze, memory replaces recollection, sleep becomes a nocturnal siesta in summer's full light. And I haven't even begun to count the alpha waves!

These concrete acts, these skin signs, the words which go with them, combine to give birth to *yearning,* like an imperative aerial vision. This space is not at all a passive observation zone in thin air; on the contrary, it incites a capacity for synthesis that is made up of the living breathing body. It is then that words must prove themselves, that rhythm is trans-

---

9. From *Amantes* (Montreal: Les Quinze, 1980), p. 49. My translation. "... (with them)" is "(avec elles)" in the original, meaning "with them (these **women**)."
10. Ibid, p. 51. My translation.

formed, that energy finds on the page the arrangement required if one is to succeed at taking on reality.

I am talking here about a certain angle of vision. To get there, I had to get up and move, in order that the opaque body of the patriarchy no longer obstruct my vision. Displaced, I am. And not like a girl who didn't quite make it but like someone they missed out on, someone they missed their shot on when they once had her in their sights for the bead of a rifle will never have at its disposal the powers of a mirror. This displacement gives rise to all the others. Displacement of sense, not to be confused with disorder of the senses. Rather, it's a matter of what engenders the senses and what arranges them, a matter of all texture called upon to concentrate itself in text. This text I imagine each time, this text I bring about at the very moment when sureness of emotion engenders fictive fire in the breast, water and ardour giving meaning to the exploration. It happens therefore that I sometimes articulate *an abstraction*.

All memory works to reconstruct the skin and the hollows of childhood, even the colour of one's labia. All memory works in space to produce its form. Gertrude Stein wrote: "It is hard not to while away the time. It is hard not to remember what this is." This was in the context of "Sentences and Paragraphs."[11] And a few lines earlier, one could read: "Analysis is a womanly word. It means that they discover there are laws."[12] "They," these women, make me dream, remind me that knowledge, as we say, brings me back to the certain fictional aspect of things and emotions which nourish the body and impel it toward other centres and other meanings. Memory signals to me from the textual side of the continent of women.

---

11. Gertrude Stein, *How to Write* (1931; rpt. West Glover, Vermont: by Something Else Press, 1973), p. 32.
12. Ibid, p. 32.

B) URBAN WOMEN RADICALS

More and more women are writing and publishing. But who are these women who give me texts which make me think, a space I can take over and inhabit, a time for rebirth in each one? I call them urban radicals. Chance, the kind no throw of the dice will ever abolish,[13] has it that they are lesbians, by their skin and by their writing. That is to say that they conceive of reality the way they envisage themselves, in the process of becoming and of exploring pleasure, rapt, concentrated on the old landscape (to better comprehend), as attentive to knowledge as to their pupils.

Women, urban radicals of writing in movement, change reality, call it back to the drawing board, the laboratory of thought. There, it is subjected to transformations essential to the survival of projects keeping us alive. Urban radicals cross cities and myths, meeting there all manner of women: ranging from the ancient neolithic Mother-Goddess all the way to today's little wife. Tchador and kitchen aprons. Amazons, witches, and learned women.

Text memory and risk memory. For the chances are great that while considering words one by one suddenly those multitudinous keys, which patriarchal oppression and its monstrous allure make manifest, will loom into view.

Devoted to thought and to analysis, urban radicals shift the question of text to fiction and the imaginary. This brings to mind, by strange coincidence, several texts from Latin America, land of torture, land where everything that speaks intelligence and sharing is exterminated.

For urban radicals, words represent what is at stake every day in combat writing. In such a manner as to expand the mental space nourishing the body, causing us to redefine

---

13. A line taken from Mallarmé's poem, "un coup de dés jamais n'abolira le hasard." My translation.

words as simple as: drowsiness, vertigo, memory, intelligence, experience.

The patriarchal universe has us all accustomed to exercising our faculties in linear fashion. Our reading of reality is conditioned throughout by the patriarchal tradition which itself constitutes reality. Our senses are trained to perceive reality through what is useful to its reproduction. Urban radicals unsettle the senses, thereby driven to a relentless exploration of sense.

Whether it is a matter of skin or a problem for linguistics, it seems to me that any meaning shift occasions a breach of reality, if only in the way we perceive this reality. If this breach is instantaneous, we can call it rupture. From one rupture to the next, we succeed in breaking linearity. But it can be newly reconstructed, as it was, as it is, fragment by fragment. In this, the work on the text will have perhaps only altered the chronological notion of writing without, for all that, having acted on its spatio-temporal relief.

When by contrast and contrariety a meaning shift produces a breach, and everything about it gives the impression that it has come to stay, the urban radical slips in the writing hand to take account of how sense breaks through to her senses. Then she slips her entire being in, concentrated on/in the opening, turns round on herself, until she discovers the curve which gives her to understand she has entered a spiral. She then applies herself to this reality, a previously unheard-of reality, difficult to believe, which becomes bit by bit fictive and then finally, fiction. Our most vital truths, do they not lie at the base of what seems obvious but what is in fact the fiction reality has moved so fast to make?

Urban radicals invent fictions which mirror them infinitely, like two and some thousand different raindrops. What they conclude about reality transforms itself into *a thinking perspective* which is the very texture of the texts they produce. Urban radicals project something resembling memory made plural, multifaceted mirrors reflected into real space. Text experienced like a three-dimensional image, instantly available, like a new skin, a skin no longer imprinted with the anecdotal symbols invented by the terror-spreading patriarchal machine.

What is unreadable, what is unlawful about urban radicals is only, all things taken into account, the plausible version of the energy of women in quest and in movement.

C) IMAGINE

One has the imagination of one's century, one's culture, one's generation, one's particular social class, one's decade, and the imagination of what one reads, but above all one has the imagination of one's body and of the sex which inhabits it. What could be more appealing to our imagination than the tenacious forms which haunt memory, mobile female forms which bring into play in us their own pulsating movement.

The imagination travels in language and through skin. The entire surface of the skin. This all begins very early, but it also takes place when the text shifts slowly between the lines, encountering en route the facets and versions which form fiction, suggesting that in reality it might actually be a new skin in the perspective of experience. When the body of the text shifts on its surface, it knows it can no longer escape its own constitution. It takes on a new posture, a posture initiated by newfound integrity. Thus does one traverse one's text, one's paper veil, as one comes through one's fictive woman in order to find there a real woman, sitting at her worktable, writing. New configuration. Words / knowledge / emotion: I foresee them simultaneously. And I come back to this.

In the present tense of the text, I imagine the emotion which relates it to its own intelligence. I intervene in my body's history, through its memory, its gathering activity: its reflection.

The female body, long frozen (besieged) in the ice of the interpretation system and in fantasies relentlessly repeated by patriarchal sex, today travels through, in its *rapprochement* to other women's bodies, previously unknown dimensions, which bring it back to its reality.

To a certain extent, it is because I am obliged by reality, and because I am initiated to what's real and its fictive version, that I shift toward the imaginary: but I bring along my text, this thought matter which serves as my inscription in the historical space to which I belong.

Imaginary and text: site of my ardour, what arouses me, what appeals to me. All this revolves around apparent meaning; what is unmistakable, and what actually manifests itself as essential to a writing project, where each coincidence of what's real and what's fictive prints on the public page the reality of this body: word still stuck in the throat. When the throat becomes valley, and the silence of valleys reaches my ear like a rumour that's true, then you have the imaginary.

Thus I inscribe: "writing is an insurmountable fiction. An insurmountable fiction refers us back to writing. That is, back to a certain facsimile of self engaged in day-to-day life," when, suspended over a major work, tuned to the timbre of voice, to local time, what unfurls is nothing other than one's raw material which, in a word, woman, burns with imagination in the same way one can be ablaze with beauty.

On all sides: thought. Enter this body, coming from the continent of the imaginary, this body enraptured in space.

The imagination travels through skin. Skin is energy. Eros is at work in all writing. How then does it proceed in the feminine? Is there a suggestion of body? Which body does it propose as partner in order that from one complicitous moment to the next the desire of the woman who writes brings about her own authentic renewal? Is this a question of body or of mental space? Furthermore, is it a question of energy, intact energy as yet unspoiled by patriarchal propaganda?

If the question of text revolves around knowledge, the question of writing revolves around energy, like a spatio-temporal zone we must work our way into, be attendant to with brain and senses combined, rhythmic.

Writing is a privileged practice of the written word which permits the dreaming of text. I say one must dream one's text, like a living organism which multiplies the apprenticeship of the reason for all existence: ecstasy and thought. To borrow the title of one of Luce Irigaray's books, let us say that one doesn't move without the other.[14] We would agree then that this amounts to an enormous task in a civilization which works toward ensuring that neither one move.

IV
THE AERIAL LETTER

Everything I've written here leads me back to its beginning, that is, to an initial utterance, which is the aerial letter. To get there, I had to pass the test of text, the test in the feminine plural memory, my women's continent, and the imaginary. I am not concluding something here, rather, I affirm an initiation route. I examine the cartography of a set of realities which, having traversed me, initiate me to the idea of an aerial vision: a fiction-writing project which would co-respond to it like an echo. The fictive version of a few ideas, the passionate quest

---

14. Luce Irigaray, *Et L'Une Ne Bouge Pas Sans L'Autre* (Paris, France: Les Editions de Minuit, 1979).

of form to render them real; that's what always ends up in my texts.

This capacity we have to live words in accordance with certain sensations in the perspective of all-inclusive thought, apt to renew desire and to see it take cultural and political form, sums up the overwhelming confrontation of the political and the personal. A question I feel I must approach by way of the aerial letter.

First of all, let us say that one enters the aerial letter just as one slips inside one's skin and into the writing which constitutes it and of which it is made. Under the influence of the aerial vision, certain zones known for their "redundant opaque clarity" cloud over; others become nuanced or illuminated. Thus, at the heart of the aerial letter, certain zones appear clear, zones we would otherwise register with difficulty, given the political vision we have of beings and the activities they participate in.

It is because the aerial vision never freezes its gaze on any one thing that it becomes possible to see the state of reality with incalculable precision. Something very precise is proposed to me here which I have to nonetheless discover then, on getting down to work, if you will. But one question still goes unanswered: in 1980, what inner resources do we have at our disposal for confronting a reality unremittingly altered to the point where it becomes logical to doubt it? For instance: What is a 'coup d'état'? What is the will of the people? Ronald Reagan, what's that? *Le Nouvel Observateur* asks – does it not – every two months, what does it mean to be French? And writers, what is literature? As if we were, one after the other, condemned to pirate the reality holographically projected onto the mental landscape of the Eighties.

With which inner resources will we survive the civilization of man, that wasteland littered with patriarchal debris?

Meanwhile, as we make use of a sensual and cerebral

capacity which lends itself to a form of original concentration, is it a fiction of history or a crisis in history, to bring its days to an end – and our's as well – in derision and the grotesque? Either way, we lose.

No matter how I look at the question, I am continually brought back to writing, not just any writing but that which I have to imagine in order to subsist, the way I dream an inexpressible reality, one which tests me, one I test and delve into deeply.

Writing is a fiction; that is why I imagine it assuming all sorts of forms inscribed in our biological rhythms, in the rhythms imposed by the environment, as well as those we choose. The aerial letter is what becomes of me (through the written word), when an emotion slowly sets to work, opening me to forms of existence other than those I have known through the anecdotes of political, cultural, sexual, or sensual mores.

The aerial letter is the fantasy which permits me to read and write in three dimensions; it is my laser. Space-time-mobility in History with this vision equipped for seeing History right down to the skin, in a manner that lets us distinguish those moments where we step out of it, moments where it is essential that, where possible, we reintegrate it, to change the course of it. To take leave of one's skin also means *to depart,* to make one's way slowly and with difficulty toward other fictions, toward that which in theory calibrates.

Writing then, as I conceive of it, with its aerial letters, is what permits me simultaneously to keep one eye on the historical anecdote (on which I depend, moreover), and one eye on the development of my global vision: cortex and skin of every gyn/ecological memory. Of every memory projected in the odyssey of mental space. From out in front, I correct the curve of my orbit, as one corrects one's text, for the sake of form.

The aerial letter literally constitutes my text, taken directly from a single and a multiple consciousness which insinuates that we are always like water and mirror, fire and matrix, like that which conquers even the principle of conquest, that is, what captivates our senses and suggests the poem which makes me say that the chest holds the meaning of the breath we find there, as if each time it were a matter of writing: I carry on.

"La Lettre aérienne" was a text written for presentation at Cerisy-la-Salle in August 1980. Passages of the following texts are to be found in: "The identity as science fiction of self," *Identités collectives et changements sociaux* (Privat, 1980); "L'épreuve de la modernité," *La Nouvelle Barre du Jour*, No. 90-91 (May 1980); "Un corps pour écrire," *Le Devoir*, 24 November 1979.

we call memory a precise form of recollection which reminds us of death fire and torture traversing female bodies death fire and torture like three horsemen let loose charged with diffusing over us the odour of the patriarchal plague. we call imagination the knowledge we have of ellipses, spirals, and the reach of the cyclic arcs, when the taste for island and the appetite for urban combat converge in our saliva. we call appetite that which kindles in us the instinct for movement, for to venture a move, one must instinctively both remember and imagine from a single appetite the physical stance and gestures of combat. we call body the form our bodies take once they have tried their hand at memory, imagination, and appetite. we call combat the time we will consecrate to reality in order to experience what's real. and combat is also the sensation of acknowledging one's emotions. this other feeling which comes over us during moments of introspection, the ones that metamorphose long explosive nights.

Le Sens apparent

CRITICAL APPRECIATION

To TALK ABOUT LITERARY criticism, one must first look at the object of criticism, writing, and the fiction it translates and makes space for.

Though we may speak of feminist texts, it seems to me that we cannot speak of feminist writing. Insofar as I conceive of writing as a way of using the body, that is, how the body physically asserts itself to gain its formal status in linguistic terrain, I can speak only of feminine and/or lesbian writing. Certainly, the body has ideas and feminist thoughts but the body itself is not feminist; if it were, you can be sure that the face of the world would have been changed accordingly. Feminism can make a place for a 'body politic' but it cannot offer us a writing of the body or of the skin. However, feminist consciousness nourishes and transforms the body's cognitive and perceptual modes.

I am thus going to have to ask the question: How does the feminine body and/or lesbian skin proceed to write fiction? To respond succinctly, I will draw on the origin of the word fiction, "fingere," which is the same as for the word feign, and I will retain its sense of imagination. I am interested, then, in two dimensions of writing: a) the movement of the imagination, that is to say, the darting gestures of thought, and b) the strategies (feints/tricks/devices) writing adopts to make the figures of the imagination materialize.

At this point, I would like to enumerate some movements used in the gestation of thought from which, it seems to me, feminine content emerges: a) oscillating movement, which manifests a certain ambivalence; b) repetitive movement, as if to exorcise the patriarchal voice; c) spiraling movement, which serves to gradually conquer the territory concerned; and d) floating movement, where thought is suspended over the void.

All writing of fiction is a strategy for confronting what is real, for transforming this reality, for inventing another one. Among the longterm strategies,† one frequently finds: a) irony, humour, and parody; b) intertextuality; c) the use of a foreign language; d) anthropomorphism; and e) the use of myths or the creation of female characters of mythic proportions, for example, *L'Euguélionne* by Louky Bersianik.

Movements and strategies of writing are related proportionally to the intensity, the urgency, and the ultimate necessity for revealing that which is believed to be essential. For women, the essential is either unutterable, unthinkable, or worse, *forbidden to thought*. The more the essential is unthinkable, that is, thwarted or repressed in non-sense (for example, that a woman love another woman, that god be a woman, and so forth), the more complex the necessary strategies. And strategies of another order must also be developed to confront the notion of the forbidden, or quite simply, *that which is forbidden*. In other words, let us say that strategies which are capable of producing sense, of inventing sense, exist where there was none (or was non-sense), while others serve to transgress patriarchal sense.

◊

What can feminist criticism do and what does it want? It seems to me that criticism cannot do more for literary texts than the texts do for themselves. By that, I mean that if, let's say, you

---

† Short-term strategies are concerned with stylistic devices.

enter the universe of Anne Hébert, you cannot function as though you were in that of Louky Bersianik or France Théoret. In all honesty, we must acknowledge that the critical environment for a text is dictated by the writing itself. And, as Louise Forsyth said, "We have to know where a woman is writing *from.*"

But what can feminist criticism do? A word that is part of the definition of "criticism" comes to mind: *appreciate.* For in appreciation, there is impression, feeling, and *evaluation.* At last! We arrive at a level of critical evaluation which will be ours, where we are able to appreciate each other reciprocally. But appreciate what? A style, a unique voice, a plural voice? *Appreciate a system of feminine values, the movement and strategies of feminine and/or lesbian writing.* Appreciate the courage of the writing, or appreciate the breakthrough in thought produced by the intellect of new women? *Appreciate, make visible, and move to the fore, that which we know to be essential to our intellectual and spiritual community.*

Let us also recognize that no critical appreciation will be exempt from strategy. In summary, these criss-crossings of networks, perspectives, and intellectual struggles in the conquest of our female territories are essential for the emergence of a culture of our own. We contribute to its expansion and extend its horizon each time we publish, each time we critique ourselves, and appreciate each other's work.

In closing, I would like to say that the critical texts which fill me with wonder are those which opt for the writing of pleasure, those which are ripe with emotion and thought. This leads me to speak briefly of the women writers and critics I call the Synchrones. More than being complicitous by circumstance, they are perfectly synchronized in the mental space of writing's thinking and desiring. Without this synchrony, this symphony, it seems to me that something essential is lost of the thought traversing both the dictionary and reality. The essential is what we seek to put into words for we do not yet have the words to say *that*. The essential is what is on the other side of the patriarchal semantic line, and that is what we have to imagine with our three-dimensional and radiant bodies, carried resplendent through the patriarchal night like fluorescent cities of visionary learned women.

"L'Appréciation critique" was read at York University, Toronto, at the "Dialogue" conference held in October 1981.

all these books you surround yourself with, I think that excites you in some vital way. me too, *for that matter, as if there were essences emanating from each book. we're playing with the invisible then. seduced, transported, irrevocably touched. we have to outsmart the strategy of books each time, leaving behind, along the thread of what we're reading, our own biographical skin.*

...

i tell you of my passion for reading you hidden behind your quotations. Facts are such that the project of text and the text of project come to fruition in the taste for words, the taste of a kiss. you are real to me and I know it/so

Amantes

Synchrony

"Reality" is what we take to be true. What we take to be true is what we believe. What we believe is based upon our perceptions. What we perceive depends upon what we look for. What we look for depends upon what we think. What we think depends upon what we perceive. What we perceive determines what we believe. What we believe determines what we take to be true. What we take to be true is our reality.

Gary Zukav
The Dancing Wu Li Masters,
An Overview of the New Physics

All this (writing, that is) remains and will continue to remain a question of consciousness, an indispensable mathematics of consciousness, a science and a fiction of self, self being what counts and what exerts itself despite the perils and risks, in order to understand everything, understand everything passionately with energy and intelligence, understand everything that happens inside oneself, *around* oneself, to make happen what can happen once we agree to let words provide reality with its surface relief, give it, in a certain sense, its volume.

To write in the year 2000 is to write here and now and yet again; and for me, the only scenario for doing this will be the very one which, in the process of writing itself, leaves traces across that film of patriarchal sediment covering words, and skirts the semantic line (to date, we have known only its patriarchal slant) so as to render visible and possible the multiple

97

uses and meanings which are there, present and available, in each word. A different perspective, different meaning, different way to read.

To write is always to make the inadmissible emerge; to produce, from the collective imaginary territory we occupy, other cues, other vehicles for thought. It is to conceive of a link between mental space, body, and reality: in sum, through the very practice of language to conceive of what is inconceivable outside language. It is to know how *to be synchronized* there.

Now the imaginary territory, on which our ideas depend and from which our impetus springs, is for the moment furrowed in all its parts by theological and philosophical slogans ("God" being the most well known, followed closely by the word "man") which, on the one hand exclude and, on the other encompass, any feminine perspective. This territory of the imaginary, founded on a single subjectivity which is masculine, and which is reproduced in social organization as reality, is no longer equal to the task. By that I mean that to think, love, imagine, and write only in this context is an undertaking one must not hesitate to identify as derisive.

◊

Writing is a consciousness formally at work in the territory of the imaginary. There, where words make images, where images take form in words, anything can happen: a sudden fever, an uncanny premonition of a strategy for keeping one's wits, or the recognition of something undeniably obvious. So that what can happen, happens: it trans/forms itself. At the turning point, some metaphors we had thought indelible are lost. Others suddenly loom into view but follow different rhythms, consciousness in/forms itself, its movement informs. On an individual level I think that this has rarely happened, but when it has it was through writing. Now, both the territory of the imaginary and one's individual consciousness are ultimately operating within new paradigms: on the one hand, that of feminist consciousness, on the other, that which could be summed up by the expression *the third wave.* "The problem is that we cannot grasp the new paradigm as long as we have not yet abandoned the old one."[1] But it is certainly true that from this time forward, time and space are altered, not only by our way of living but also by the new way we have to fantasize them, maybe fantasize is no longer even the appropriate word.

To write in the year 2000 and now is definitely to learn how to think the unimaginable, the inconceivable, from the moment when deep inside we feel absolutely certain about what is indisputably obvious. It will not be a question of writing like they did in 1900 (if we think of the best of that literature) and neither will it be like writing in the year 1982 (in the contemporary literary scene). To write now and in the year 2000 means: to write what has never before been thought in the history of *Man's memory.*

Between then and now, the body transforms itself, as do the metaphors which, while they enhance the body, also immobilize it. Thus we are witnessing the appearance of entirely new metaphors, some associated with the brain: the hologram, the computer. We are witnessing that, of the four elements, AIR is becoming even more important, or at least as important as earth, water, and fire, which are more concrete. We will see the *heart* let the whole *body* discover its reasons. And what to say about the eye whose *outlook* on the world is no longer enough to give rise to a *vision.* It must be said too that the history of the gaze has changed since women have opened their eyes and that *touching,* this sense we have so long confused with "lay your hands on," impresses upon each skin cell that it must work at the emotion of living. Yes, it really must be said that by taking back their body through writing, women confront writing, that is, they bring it face to face with what has never before come to mind: the ontological exis-

---

1 Marilyn Ferguson. *Les Enfants du Verseau* (Paris: Calmann-Lévy, 1981), p. 99.

tence of women. Needless to say, the more words are diverted from the patriarchal stream, the more fulfilling will be thought, emotion, dictionaries, and cities.

I must say that I expect this to have a deeply disturbing effect on whoever will be working/is working within a terminology which mistakes woman for nature in terms of hunting, fishing, and fertility, on whoever confuses heat with light, on whoever tangles up man and woman in the same slogan, on whoever confuses their birth with their name.

It must also be said that to write in the year 2000 is to know that as the fantasized space concerning death, heterosexuality, the infinitely small, the infinitely large, becomes smaller, as these fields become smaller, others, linked to this in body but which cannot yet claim to embody knowledge, open up. It is without a doubt what I once used to call the unimaginable.

I thus come to imagine myself hologram, actual, virtual, three-dimensional in the imperative of coherent light. Yes, I imagine more and more, times being what they are, that fiction brings us closer and closer to what resembles the energy bodies we are. Or maybe, at its most crucial moment, fiction is simply a premonitory feeling of the knowledge we can have of energy processes that think us and that we think. In any case, I would say that if there is a *term* for fiction, it surely has yet to be invented.

◊

In short: the 31st of December 1999, when at midnight I open a bottle of champagne, you can be sure that, at that very instant, my page will be white, like the first page you see when you open a book.

"Synchronie" was written for the "10e Rencontre québécoise international des écrivains," held in April, 1982. It was published in *Le Devoir* as part of the feature, "Ecrire en l'an 2000," 17 April 1982.

it was a fabulator problem for a woman who wanted the word woman to take its own place and be in place yet still be able to drift away in the split-second moment of composing image or so that in silence she could think of her marvels and when the moment was just right roll herself up around civilization like new mores aspiraling to nothing so much as to write in the per-fected expanse of the brain

but words confuse silence and ardour   even   in inertia in one's work room the gazebyfar serves the inexplicable will to sojourn, this was to write patience and its effects underscored with violence

Domaine d'écriture

FROM RADICAL
TO INTEGRAL

if patriarchy can take what exists and make it not, surely we can take what exists and make it be. But for this we have to want her in our own words, this very real integral woman we are, this idea of us, which like a vital certitude, would be our natural inclination to make sense of what we are.

To attest to the emergence of, or to critically examine a female culture in the context of millennia and the present patriarchal civilization, is a project I can only envision around a single expression: *to make sense*. For as soon as we speak of culture, we necessarily speak of codes, signs, exchanges, communication, and recognition. Likewise, we must speak of a system of values which, on the one hand, determines what makes sense or non-sense and which, on the other, normalizes sense so that eccentricity, marginality, and transgression can be readily identified as such, in order to control them if need be. In other words, I would like here to touch upon the question of sense and non-sense, where perceptions, desires, reality, fiction, and ideology meet, cancel each other out, or transform one another. For nothing is ever lost of what makes sense or non-sense; it could all culminate in a straitjacket or it could be put to good use in creative work. In other words, once again I will have to make text of my body, focused on the patriarchal system and its tenacious will to endure in us, keeping us on the out/side of the magic of words. By the magic of words, I mean that which proceeds to elaborate thought and its emotion, that which transforms, which motivates being, the being I am or she who I could be, or further still, she who I desire to be to the point of becoming her in an unalienable present, to the point of being what happens to me, that is, what I am.

I
LIFE IN THE ONE-WAY SENSE

Between Simone de Beauvoir's expression, "One is not born a woman, one becomes one" and Jacques'[1] "Woman does not exist," the semantic effect of the word *woman* allows us to think that, one way or the other, to speak of *woman* is something which is appropriate only in a so-called fictional environment or, to return to the etymological sense of the word *fiction,* in a realm of pretence and deceit. If the content of these two affirmations seems to be in agreement, "woman is a fiction," those who produced them certainly are not. While Simone de Beauvoir's statement is the product of a search ending in the painful recognition of the non-existence of woman as being, Jacques' statement is the repetition of a proven political formula; men's good fortune proves it.

Woman, in the one-way sense, would thus be a word having only a patriarchal root. For there, at the root of words, lies what we believe exists.

---

1. Jacques Lacan, French psychoanalyst and theoretician.

A) HAVING AN ACCENT

Rooted in foreign semantic earth, we have made a substance (Man) our own without understanding that the root is "what grows in the opposite direction from the stalk." *Root* also means "the irreducible element of a word, obtained by the elimination of all *inflections* and *grammatical markers* and which constitutes a *base for meaning.*" Which amounts to saying in the analogy I have chosen to establish, that the man-root exists as base for meaning *only* in so far as all the elements of our social, perceptual, intellectual, and sexual development are eliminated from discourse. Moreover, man is root only if the grammatical markers of our existence are suppressed – and here I am, of course, thinking of the silent 'e' in French, as well as all the 'feminitudes' systematically dispossessed by the masculine, or worse yet, neutralized to the masculine.

The greatest achievement of patriarchy is to have caused, through the force of code, law, and then by habit, a situation where each woman takes patriarchal semantic substance as her own. This has not, however, altered the fact that whether well assimilated, poorly assimilated, or not assimilated at all, this foreign language which inhabits us so familiarly, is spoken by all of us women with *an accent*. Furthermore, it is by this accent that we are able to recognize one another without, for all that, necessarily understanding each other. It is therefore not with words that we will recognize each other in the first instance, for we are still incapable of taking ourselves at our word, in other words, seriously.

No, it is by our *accent,* that is, in our divergence from the norm, a spirant divergence marked by *an increase in intensity* when using certain words with certain sounds, for this accent is expressive. Among us, there is still not enough *rapproche-*

ment, the result of a collective practice of semantic divergence. At the accent stage, there are not yet any feminists. Rather, there are women here and there, isolated, ill-instructed by men, that is, ill-literate, either strong and courageous or weak and weary.

What I have just said would have made no sense (in terms of direction and movement) if women's recognition of one another by the intensity of their accent were not followed up by diligent association with one another. Associating with other women increases the intensity in each one of us, as if each woman were making ready to unveil the volume that lives within her, that circumscribes her.

B) THE INTENSITY

Now with intensity will I root myself in the place that resembles me. Now with intensity will I initiate myself to other women. The roots are aerial. The light which nourishes them, nourishes, at the same time, the tender shoots (the culture) and the root. The root is integral and aerial, the light coherent.

Can intensity give rise to semantic divergence? Will it enable the heart of our thinking to one day be written out in full? Does it give courage? Is intensity intention?

Intensity is like a strength with which we exceed the norm, the ordinary. When we say, "I have outdone my thoughts," or "words have outdone my thinking," what do we mean to say, we who have been steeped in patriarchal fiction, accustomed to keeping quiet about our perceptions, our intuitions, our most vital certitudes? *Outdo:* "To leave in back of or behind oneself while going faster"/"to go beyond what is possible or imaginable." But how does one succeed in getting ahead of one's thinking with foreign words?

106

What characterizes people who have an accent is that they distort sounds, and consequently each time they speak a foreign language they may create misunderstandings, ambiguities, even non-sense. As well, they may very well accentuate, that is, emphasize, what in principle is out of place, what theoretically is not done.

It doesn't take much for *god* to become *dog*, and it takes nothing, in French, for "she is as named" to be heard as "she is like a man."[2] The magic of words is also this way with which, and this 'what' with which we can transform reality or the sense we give to it.

C) DIFFERENCES

Now, the magic of words is given to intense women but regardless how intense women are, differences between them have previously – have they not? – been identified. Differences related to having correctly assimilated the foreign language (making good use of the dictionary, grammar, and syntax), poorly assimilated the foreign language (using words incorrectly), or not having assimilated the foreign language (lacking vocabulary, not subordinating her words, and not establishing contact with the aid of expressive collage).

These differences are not without consequence for the sense we give to words. Thus, for example, we might imagine three formulations on which to base the definition of the word *woman:* a woman is a man, a woman is a woman, a woman is what I am. Three ways then of intervening in the word *woman:* synonymous (N.B.: a synonym "serves to avoid a repetition"), tautological (N.B.: a tautology is a "flaw in form"), and polysemic (because the *I am* spoken by each woman has a different meaning). This is also a matter of conjugating the verb *to be* in several different tenses. But at this

---

2. "Elle est comme on nomme" and "Elle est comme un homme." (p. 92)

stage, whatever expression we choose in order to define ourselves, and by the very fact of defining the word *woman,* each
one of us is radically convinced that the expression she uses
makes sense of *her life* and consequently of *life in general.*
Yes, each expression indeed makes sense but it is strange that
while each formulation marks a different approach to
women's self-perception, all three converge in the same
sense: one-way sense.

A Woman is a Man

As much as this expression rings false to the ear and to what
we might understand by it, I believe that if we internalize it as
true, it is because it has been subliminally transmitted to us as
our only chance to participate in the social ritual (i.e. discourse, knowledge, politics, etc.). The will to participate
would explain our feeling that we have the right and even the
duty to claim – in the name of Man – justice, freedom, frater-
nity, equality. This would also explain why so many women
prefer to engage in political struggle as Québécois, or as work-
ers,[3] rather than to take political action as feminists.

A Woman is What I Am

This is another definition of self-as-woman which implies that
it is in the name of humanity (that is, in the name of the Man
lying dormant in us) that we can lay claim to autonomy, subjectivity, individualism, and creativity. "A woman is what I
am" also explains why so many creative women have refused,
and still refuse, to identify themselves with women. Do not
many women poets, artists, filmmakers, psychologists, sociol-
ogists, etc., say (in fine masculine form) that art and science
have no gender?

------

3. As distinct from "Québécoises" and "women who work."

Thus we have at the outset two formulas which root women in Man and which assure him a solidarity worthy of his name.

A Woman is a Woman

If this expression is a flaw in form which refers us back to biology, or, for want of something better, allows us to lay claim to a difference which has been only too systematized in inverse proportion to our energies, what humanity can we find here? What woman would want to take the risk of being a woman, a fiction she did not originate? In the environment which encircles her, woman does not exist, meaning she does not figure into sense. Outside the environment which encircles her, she appears as non-sense. This is then tantamount to saying that whoever aspires to humanity could not know how to identify with women, much less take up their common cause. Now it happens that some women have set about claiming the opposite. We call them radical feminists and their humanity is found precisely there, in the conquest they make, word by word, body to body, of the being, *woman.*

Therefore, were it not for a radical feminist consciousness intersecting the word *woman,* each of the three expressions would result in a reinforcement of patriarchal one-way sense.

In investing the word *woman* with feminist consciousness, women who are radical feminists put their finger on the button which gives access to the magic of words.

II
THE EXPLOSION OF SENSE

A) EXCITED SENSE

The general excitement of women confronted with excited sense excites the thought of emotion and the emotion of intensity. In the excitement, one cries "Preserve our roots," another, "Let's tear them all up," while another says nothing but trembles throughout her entire being. Sense oscillates. Each woman who participates in this excitement is at the height of her being. The vertigo is great. The root, aerial.

Thus intense, diverse, and gathered together, women exchange their views by means of words which are foreign to their perception, to their experience, and in this itself have difficulty agreeing on the meaning to give to words and, consequently, to their lives and their projects. In the course of these *exchanges,* certain words become devoid of meaning, some take form, others produce unexpected effects, while still others are used with extreme precision. This is revolution, in the sense that it is heady turmoil, but it is also – for each word – a revolution around its axis: we examine the root from all angles, from every point of view. It is a general excitement.

The etymology of *excite* begins with "excitare," which means "to set in motion." The word *excite* also means "to provoke (something)" and "to incite." What is going to count and be recounted at this stage of general excitement is, above all, the polyvalent value with which words will become imbued. Polyvalence because situated where we women are coming from – multiple and different – we make ambiguous use of several words and this ambiguous usage, born of our ambivalence with regard to sense, amounts to our collectively diverging temporarily from the usual meaning of words. "One-way thinking" falters under a continuous onslaught of words going off in all directions. It is this unfurling of polyvalent and multi-directional words which is going to make way for:

1. Exploding one-way sense
   shattering the concept of man as universal
   interrupting the circle of femininity
2. Producing a void, a mental space which, little by little, will become invested with our subjectivities, thus constituting an imaginary territory, where our energies will begin to be able to take form.

This stage of exploding sense is, in some ways, crucial: in fact it is at this stage that everything could either culminate in a straitjacket or be put to use in creative work. This is where one becomes or does not become a radical feminist; this is where we move back into patriarchal parameters – ready to permit ourselves a few transgressions (for women, this always costs) – or where we abandon them for unknown and unlimited spaces; this is where we leave behind our fragmented women's garb so that we can become *integral women;* this is where we quit the circle in order to enter into the spiral, that is, where the power of our energy takes form, is cultivated, is transmitted, is renewed. This is where we say good-bye, patriarchal woman, valiant shadow in the light of high noon. This is where I take the imaginary earth out from under your imagined feet. The root is aerial. The light coherent. I take it all away, for I know all there is of us: the whole. It is here where sense begins to be made. The origin is not the mother, but the sense I make of words, and originally I am a woman.

III
I MAKE SENSE OF LIFE

at the point of becoming in an inalienable present, at the point of being what I am, life. I speak in I to assure the permanence of us. If I do not assume what in me says we, the essence of what I am would live for only a lifetime, mine, and that is too short for us.

We have seen previously that, caught between the sense we give to reality and the non-sense patriarchal reality constitutes for us, we are most often forced to adapt our lives to simultaneous translation of the foreign tongue. This posture is uncomfortable. Our balance precarious. The environment hostile. How then *to make sense collectively?* For this is what is at stake, I think, when we discuss female culture. How to ensure the exchanges between us, how to circulate our thoughts, our bodies, our emotions – in short, our subjectivity – in such a way as to be able to conjugate it in objectivity? It takes at least a minimal agreement on the meaning we give to words to be able to contemplate the emergence of a culture which reflects us. I call this minimal agreement the territory of our imaginary, from which we can take flight.

While in the first instance, the activation of our differences confronting one-way patriarchal sense resulted in the explosion of sense and its void, from this point forward, we have to envisage our differences as stemming from a primary sense that has come from us. In other words, the differences issuing from patriarchal sense have given rise to *a movement,* while the differences issuing from us as the original centre will give rise to *the emergence of female culture.*

A) THE TERRITORY OF THE IMAGINARY

This territory would thus be constituted by female subjectivity traversed by a feminist consciousness. What I am naming feminist consciousness is none other than our humanity. The illusion of our humanity is everywhere, and undoubtedly this is why very few women until today have taken the trouble to look for, much less achieve, their humanity. One day humanity was lifted from us (and this is no metaphor). I remind you that for centuries we had no soul and that, in Canada, we became persons only in 1929. About our humanity, we know little more than our life-experience in the patriarchal system. Our memory is short, our heroines rare and camouflaged by censure, our senses impaired by our conditioning for self-sacrifice. They say that the unconscious is without words. What will humanity's unconscious have to say when we finally speak our humanity? It remains to be seen and heard. And remember, the territory of our imaginary is hidden in mythology, knowledge, and art. It all belongs to us. And left to us is the task of sorting out what belongs to humanity and what belongs to the conceited, megalomaniac, violent subjectivity of man. Where our humanity begins, everything begins: there where the first spire of the spiral of female culture begins, spiral of female culture where each spire would be a constituent part of a civilization spiral – for which nothing has prepared us if not the shattering of the circle provoking the very first spire.

B) ENERGY

The emergence of female culture depends on the energy we have/will have at our disposal but above all it depends on the energy we will generate, the solidarity in our common will to change the world. At the present time, we generate acts, words, and thought which still make do with the linear / binary patriarchal mentality. I speak of energy because the spiraling emergence of female culture is directly related to the mental image we make, and will continue to make, of ourselves as a source of energy for other women, and of the form which our energized interactions will take in the social, political, and intimate spheres.

Personally I don't think female culture will be either viable over the long term in a linear/binary thought system (by that I mean that it engenders other spires), or able to overcome the atrocities of a dialectic knowledge founded on patriarchal reason.

Rather, the vitality of female culture seems to me related to a system of thought and perceptions which would bring together simultaneously, in three-dimensional forms, the objects of our thought, which until now we have been forced to see only on the surface, without really knowing their volume. It is from the volume of our thought that *integral women*[4] rises up.

---

4. In *La Lettre aérienne* Brossard brings about a collective presence in "l'intégrales," a singular noun populated by the plural collective subjectivity of all integral radical feminists, that is, those who have become complete or whole.

C) INTEGRAL WOMEN

The integral women is radical. My senses origynate in her. She shares in their integrity. Time, space, belong to her; she is female symbol for all of us, "symbola," a reconnaissance sign of recognition. Figure, image, metaphor, with the meaning she gives to words, she always makes and in/core/porates sense. The light is coherent. When I saw you right in the middle of a sentence, it occurred to me I was naturally inclined toward you, as real as the idea I have of us, as real as the energy which speaks me emerging from our life stories.

"De radical à intégrales" was presented at the conference, "L'émergence d'une culture au féminin," at the University of Montreal in 1982. Another English translation appeared in *Trivia*, No. 5 (Fall 1984).

AERIAL VISION

The SPIRAL's sequences in its energy and movement
towards a female culture

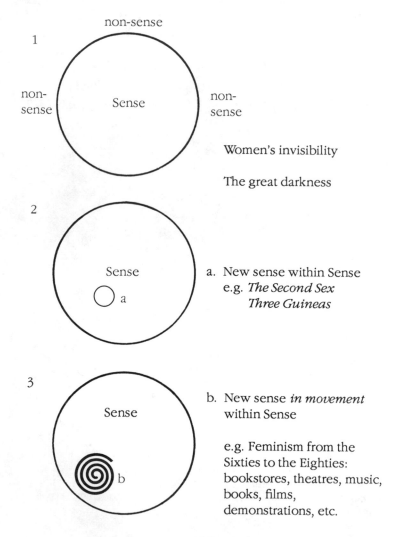

1

non-sense

non-sense   Sense   non-sense

Women's invisibility

The great darkness

2

Sense
a

a. New sense within Sense
   e.g. *The Second Sex*
        Three Guineas

3

Sense
b

b. New sense *in movement*
   within Sense

   e.g. Feminism from the
   Sixties to the Eighties:
   bookstores, theatres, music,
   books, films,
   demonstrations, etc.

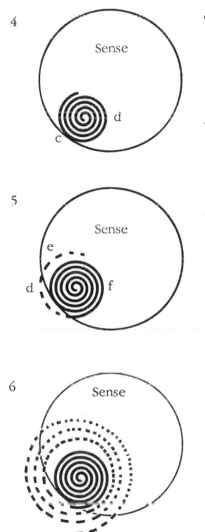

4

Sense

d

c

c. Work done on the imaginary, language, thought, and knowledge

Dangerous zone: madness, delirium, or genius

d. Radical feminism, political, economic, cultural, social, ecological, and technological feminism

5

Sense

e

d

f

d. *Questing* sense, born of the conquest of non-sense

e. Sense *renewed,* through excursions into and explorations of non-sense

f. New perspectives: new configurations of woman-as-being-in-the-world of what's real, of reality, and of fiction

6

Sense

Female culture, whose existence essentially depends on our incursions into the territory until today held by non-sense. Without sequences 5 and 6, the spiral, repressed in the borderlines of sense, would end up closing in on itself.

*Time becomes process in the ultraviolet. I am the thought of a woman who encompasses me and who I think integral. **SKIN** (UTOPIA) gesture will come. Revolve aerial and sharp the shore of suspended isles. I will be tempted then by reality which, like a verbal vision, alternates my senses while another woman takes command of working the horizon.*

utopia integral woman

*Gesture will come: a sign I would trace, a letter which would reflect me in two different voices I would be radically thinking like a shaft of light, irrigating the root, the absolute reality. The generic body would become the expression of woman and woman would have wings high up above everything; she would make a sign. Plunged deep in the city's centre, I would contemplate looking up. WOMAN **SKIN** TRAJECTORY.* Donna lesbiana dome of knowledge and volutes, I would have already started in a spiral and my air-being aerial urban would reproduce itself as a point of origin in the glass city. I would then see this woman, manifestly formal, inscribe reality, the ecosystem.

Picture Theory

KIND SKIN MY MIND

When I am writing, I decide on one word over another, one image over another. For this text, I decided on a single word only: lesbian, and the text followed – for the lesbian is *the intuition* of the most daring lucidity.

The *lesbian* is a *woman* ablaze who is reborn from the essential of what she knows (she) is. The lesbian knows the fire and the ashes of desire, of being, and of fragment; once she is reborn, anything can happen with her as gynergic centre. The ideal lesbian is ideal like the emotion and vital utopia of what makes sense and non-sense. The lesbian is an initiator, an instigator.

There are lesbians like this, lesbians like that, lesbians here, and there, but a lesbian is above all else the centre of a captivating *image* which any woman can claim for herself. The lesbian is a mental energy which gives breath and meaning to the most positive of images a woman can have of herself. Lesbians are the *poets* of the humanity of women and this humanity is the only one which can give to our collectivity a sense of what's real.

The lesbian is a threatening *reality* for reality. She is the impossible reality realized which reincarnates all *fiction,* chanting and enchanting what we are or would like to be.

The lesbian rejects *mortification* as a way of life. The lesbian suffers because of the mortification of women.

The lesbian is a woman who precedes women in women's existence. She is an explorer, an anarchist, a *feminist* who, with her body, invents everything by the force of the attraction she has for other women.

A lesbian is a woman for whom joy, suffering, or ecstasy is THE joy, THE suffering, THE ecstatic bliss. And because so named, these become the real forum for THE poetry, THE philosophy, THE reality, THE fiction. The lesbian: she who can create for the collectivity of women a sense of what's real, *the feeling of true in the positive.*

The lesbian makes patriarchal dogma invalid. The lesbian creates space and time; she is always of another time. She is a calendar, she might be a date, but most of all, **she is your memory.**

The political lesbian burns across the expanse before her. A lesbian is a woman who burns with imagination the way one smoulders with the desire for beauty, the way women's beauty sweeps through us like wild-fire.

Any lesbian is unbearable because she deceives, offends, or invalidates patriarchal sense. She defies common sense. She can make you crazy with happiness, or mad with horror.

The lesbian is living proof of women's "genius." All women would like to believe in the "genius" of women but only lesbians believe in it, take inspiration from it, live it. To believe in *Woman,* through women, is a philosophical act to which lesbians are the only women to have shown themselves disposed.

The lesbian takes part in all *tongue energy* each time she finds with the tongue of another lesbian the energy of language. A lesbian is *radical* or she is not a lesbian. A lesbian who does not reinvent the word is a lesbian in the process of disappearing.

The lesbian is the intuition of what we are *certain* of.

"Kind skin my mind" appeared in *Resources for Feminist Research/ Documentation sur la recherche féministe (RFR/DRF)* [Toronto] 12, No. 1 (March 1983).

my continent, I mean to speak the radical
effect of light in broad daylight
today, I held you close,
beloved of all civilization, all
texture, all geometry, and glowing
embers
delirious, the way we write: and
my body is enraptured

Excerpted from the poem "Ma continent," in Amantes[1]

.

___

1. Brossard's "continent" refers to the "continent of women" and in the
   original, she makes this (masculine) noun feminine (p.111).

A CAPTIVATING IMAGE

THE WOMAN IN THE IMAGE is exposed to anyone's gaze, just as to any danger in the street, at any time of the day but, to look at her, you can't tell that anything is wrong; she always has the same *affected* air. It costs her her body, this lack of naturalness. The woman in the image affects the existence of women, designates women to reproduction.

The woman in the image is a fake who has caused a lot of ink to flow, and has provoked that stony urge to start over again. The woman in the image carries a child, or would. One way to talk about this would be to take inventory of her poses, but even then the illusion would still not be dispelled.

The image of woman is a foreign body in the eye of man. Fatally, man fixes in his memory "strange, incomprehensible" woman. It follows that the imitation is a "kind of."

Invisibility is a woman in a book.

WOMAN

Numerous they may be, but fixed images in painting and photography, and animated images in cinema or in the mind, bear explicit (for the most part) or implicit witness that woman is linked, unconditionally, body and soul, to the male of the human species. And the use of woman as symbol is For Men Only: woman as nature, death, horror, sometimes victory, justice, wisdom, or even liberty. Men are impressed by muses, witches, medusas, sirens, and Gorgons.

A symbol sparks recognition. The woman in the image, do I recognize myself in her? Does she signal to me? Does she hold for me a sense so precious that in my eyes she becomes *a captivating image,* so captivating that all my attention, all my energy, is devoted to her?

In the present patriarchal state of things, I will reply that woman is a captivating image to the extent that I imagine her from what in me speaks true, that is, from what doesn't ring false.

To imagine woman would be to establish an ontological analogy between her (she doesn't exist yet) and me (I exist). Then the idea behind this first analogy could branch out into a network of images, each one more concrete than the next, all of them so concrete that I see this image everywhere in humanity.

But for this to happen, I first have to invent who I am; while I'm in the process of imagining this, I have to think and invent myself into existence.

◊

The image's ultimate power is to reflect, or to incite reflection, for I cannot, me, woman, find my essence reflected in a body which is *formally* alien to me, as foreign to me as a body-concept which sees, desires, and looks for death in woman so that to it will be given life – my own no less.

Now it happens that this Man-made body-concept, assisted by language, religions, mythologies, art, and science, succeeds in being so thoroughly reflected in and by woman that, out loud, she thinks she's a Man, so resoundingly that not one of us has time to recognize herself, except in silence.

How then am I to imagine woman? When I say *imagine woman,* surely it will have been understood that I mean *imagine the world,* that is, give to the universe meaning which partakes of the intelligence I have of me, woman in the world.

If I am a patriarchal woman, that is, a woman who espouses the sense Man makes of life, which encompasses woman, it follows from two things, one alone: either I repeat after Man or I think new thoughts but in male-stream sense. Either way, that amounts to *the same thing,* and unavoidably *what's essentielle*[1] escapes me, dis-integrates, and slips through my fingers. Each time a woman's essential self-image escapes her, Man is reaffirmed in collective memory; Man reinforces a collective imagination we know to be destructive for women.

If, on the other hand, I am displaced in relation to patriarchal sense, in other words out of line (and in this lies my only hope of being), that is, if from where I am, the words of the patriarchy no longer *impress* me, I am literally forced to compose, to imprint in space, an image of myself which can represent me, which makes me present by exposing me, as I believe myself to be.

Sooner or later, what is new and original in my self-image of woman (this is also what is hoped for) meets up with the eyes of another woman. My eyes come across another woman: I recognize at last the essentielle. I identify / myself. The image starts to look appealing (acceleration velocity); its general appearance is transformed. I believe this is also what we call a very attractive proposition. Djuna Barnes wrote in *Nightwood,* "One's life is particularly one's own when one has invented it."[2] This suits me perfectly; I find it delightful.

◊

I would like now to speak of images and women in terms of environment, context, and information. For the body which is formally familiar to me, like a concept at work in a book, an

---

1. *Elle* means *she* in French.
2. Djuna Barnes, *Nightwood* (1936; rpt. London: Faber and Faber, 1963), p. 169.

image, or a street, is currently enjoying a wide range of expression.

"Tell me who you associate with and I'll tell you who you are."

The image we have of ourselves is narrowly linked to the image flashed back at us by our immediate environment and the socio-cultural environment (advertizing, film, television, art, etc.). Likewise, the images we project of ourselves are read, interpreted, accepted, or rejected according to a set of values that determines how they are received, the importance they are accorded, and subsequently the reprobation or approbation given. And few are the people who remain indifferent to gratification or sanction.

It goes without saying then that if I project an image of myself, woman, which goes against what is expected (of course, we are allowed to be a little racy), chances are good that it will meet with disapproval. At the very worst, one would be censored, rejected, or forced to endure a reproachful silence.

For women, practicing the identity of the self (to borrow an expression from Marisa Zavalloni) generally takes place in a hostile environment, the consequence of which, in the short and middle run, will be silence or even deceit (one negotiates the possibility of a fake image with oneself ... in the way one plays dead, one contrives femininity). It is necessary, therefore, if one wishes to pursue the most precise image possible of self and to disclose it, that one live in such a way as to associate with those beings who resemble us sufficiently to create *a connection* (affinity, rapport, liaison, analogy). This way, there is a sequel to who I am, to who we are.

Associating with women who have a captivating image of themselves is an indispensable condition for having a captivating image of one's own self; *essentielle to,* as it were.

Women associating with other women is an image in itself which holds my attention for it informs and inspires me. It is directly related to the production and creation of sense, and to the image of woman I invent by projecting me, by projecting my identity, in space.

THE CONQUEST OF SPACE: CONTEXT

context: from *contextus,* which means "assemblage." from *contexer,* which means "to weave with."

"The textual whole which surrounds an element of language (a word, a sentence, a part of a statement), and from which we derive its meaning, its importance."

1. Context is *information* as such, and no one escapes it for this information subliminally colours our perception, our reading. Context also provides a meaningful arena for interpretation. And it is from context that a given reality, image, or word takes on one sense rather than another, or yet again, makes no sense at all. Context can restrain our attention or modify our perception, just as it can also stir us with unforeseen inexpressible images .

Thus, in the framework of a women's film festival, or an exhibition, such as the one which brought together *La chambre nuptiale, The Dinner Party,* and *Art et féminisme,* it would be pointless to claim that the reading we make of these works is not influenced by the fact that we are very pleased these women artists are occupying so much space. Consciously or unconsciously, we experience a sense of belonging which stimulates in us a series of free associations which now revives our anger, now renews our solidarity, now freshens our imagination. Invigorated, we are women's creative energy gathered together.

It would be interesting someday to examine the effects of the images we produce: exact reflection, caricature (exaggeration of features), symbolic image of our patience and our repeated gestures, images prepared and dealt out from consciousness. What are the images which best lend themselves to a grasp of conscious awareness? Which ones give the sweet desire to start over (associated with creation)? How, by what means is desire mediated? What are its *motifs*? Its *motives*?

2. Context is *inspiration*. The information we acquire about ourselves from the context that we give ourselves gradually becomes inspiration, that is, *breath* and *enthusiasm*. This inspiration restores to the community of women their energy. The energy of each captivating woman activates women's energy, and it is from this energy that a collective consciousness of who we are is born.

Who we are and who we will become is essentially dependent on how well we are able to produce stimulating images of ourselves, images which literally excite us. It is clear that the *affected air* we have had for centuries will not be done away with overnight, but our analysis and interpretation of this affectation will (from here on in) make it impossible to transmit this air as though it were natural.

Having started with a preconceived image of ourselves, we are now beginning to conceive of who we are. The word conception here has the advantage of recalling the body as well as the idea we make of it. With this body I am given to think and think it I do: virtual image, actual image, in three-dimensions. Skin reflects its origins. That an image of woman totally capture our attention; that would suffice.

"Une image captivante" is the text of a lecture given at the Musée d'art contemporain in the context of the *Art et féminisme* exhibition in Montreal in 1982. It appeared in the journal, *Amazones d'hier/lesbiennes d'aujourd'hui,* Vol. 4, no. 1 (July 1985).

*A brilliant flash of light, the astonishing wonder today that energy, the live affirmation of mental territory, is space at the turning point of the cosmic breast. I EVOKE. I CERTIFY MY HOPE. **SKIN** utopia slow vertigo. I work in the context of our body fluorescence already written. I perform the rites and the temptation of certitude in order that it branch out. I see formal woman opening onto sense for I know that each image of woman is vital in the thinking organism —— gyno-cortex. At the end of the patriarchal night, the body foresees itself in the horizon before me on a skin screen, mine, where resonance endures in that which weaves the web <u>the light</u> when beneath my tongue ripples the world's reason. M.V. was saying yes. In her eyes it was epidermal, this desire for the aerial circulation of spatial gestures initiated by the letter.**Skin**.*

Picture theory

LESBIANS OF LORE

IN THE FIRST PLACE, not everyone is a writer and not all women are lesbians. We are dealing here with two modes of existence which inscribe themselves in the margins of the normal-normative course of language and the imaginary and, consequently, in the margins of reality and fiction.

Before going any further, I would like to propose that we study this question: what is necessary in order to write? Of course, I could ask: what does it mean, to write? But it seems to me more pertinent – given our subject – to try to answer the first question, which to a certain extent has bearing on the identity of lesbian writers.

Generally speaking, I would say that in order to write one must a) know that one exists, b) have a captivating and positive self-image, and c) respond to the inner necessity – if only in self-defense – to inscribe one's perception and one's vision of the world in language. In other words, one must have the desire, be it conscious or not, to make one's presence known, to declare one's existence in the world. Finally, one must: d) feel a profound dissatisfaction with the prevailing and mainstream discourse, which denies differences and obstructs thought.

In sum, then, to write is to be a subject in process: moving, changing, a being in pursuit of. To write, you must first belong to yourself.

We could, at this point, conclude that writing, its practice, is a subject that concerns the individual first and foremost. But as

Jean Piaget so aptly remarks, "One who has not had a sense of a potential plurality has absolutely no awareness of his or her own individuality."[1] This means that in order to be conscious of oneself as an individual, as someone unique in the world, what must come first is an acknowledgement of one's belonging to a group or a collectivity. Whatever our ethnic or religious origins, we all belong quite visibly to the category "women." What characterizes women as a group is our colonized status. To be colonized is not to think for oneself, to think on behalf of "the other," to put one's emotions to work in the service of "the other." In short, not to exist. Above all, one is unable to find in one's own group those sources of inspiration and motivation essential to all artistic production. It is crucial that we find in our own group captivating images which can nourish us spiritually, intellectually, and emotionally. What and who inspire women? What and who then inspire lesbians? Integrally, in a non-fragmented manner. In fact, perhaps we should distinguish between what motivates us and what inspires us. Thus, I could say that women motivate me because as a woman and feminist among women, I have a profound motivation to change the world, to change language and to change society. I could also say that lesbians inspire me in the sense that we are a challenge for the imagination and, in a certain way, a challenge for ourselves, to the extent that we give birth to ourselves in the world. Only through literally creating ourselves in the world do we declare our existence and from there make our presence known in the order of the real and the symbolic.

When I say literally give birth to ourselves in the world, I really do mean that literally. *Literal* means "that which is represented by letters." Taken literally. Taken to the letter. For we do take our bodies, our skin, our sweat, pleasure, sensuality,

---

1. Quoted by Edgar Morin in *L'Homme et la mort,* Collection Point, No. 77 (Paris: Seuil, 1976), p. 112.

sexual bliss to the letter. From the letters forming these words emerge the beginnings of our texts. We also take our energy and our cleverness to the letter, and we make of our desire a spiral which delivers us into the movement toward sense. Sense which originates with us. Not a counter-sense, a misinterpretation, which would have us trailed in tow throughout the patriarchal universe, like so many tiny stars. Symbolically, and realistically, I think only women and lesbians will be able to legitimize a trajectory toward the origin and future of sense, a sense that we are bringing about in language.

To be at the origin of sense means that we project to the world something resembling what we are and what we dis/cover about ourselves, unlike the patented version of women which patriarchal marketing has made of us, on posters and in person.

To write, for a lesbian, is to learn how to take down the patriarchal posters in her room. It means learning how to live with bare walls for a while. It means learning how not to be afraid of the ghosts which assume the colour of the bare wall. In more literary terms, it means renewing comparisons, establishing new analogies, braving certain tautologies, certain paradoxes. It means starting one's first sentence a thousand times over: "a rose is a rose,"[2] or to think with Djuna Barnes that "an image is a stop the mind makes between uncertainties."[3] To take the risk of having too much to say or not enough. To take the chance of not finding the right words to say with precision what only we can imagine. To risk everything for the universe that takes shape between the words, a universe which, without this passion we have for the other woman, would remain a dead letter.

I think that wild love between two women is so totally

---

2. Gertrude Stein.
3. Djuna Barnes, *Nightwood* (1936; rpt. New York: New Directions Paperbook No. 98, 1961), p. 111.

inconceivable that, to talk or write *that* in all its dimensions, one almost has to rethink the world, to understand what it is that happens to us. And we can rethink the world only through words. Lesbian love therefore seems to me intrinsically a love that largely goes beyond the framework of love. Something inside us and yet beyond us – now there's an enigma for writing and fiction but, especially, for poetry.

That being said, it seems to me that for lesbians to come abreast of who they are, what they need is a bed, a worktable to write on, and a book. A book we must read and write at the same time. This book is unpublished but we are already quite familiar with its substantial preface. In it, we find the names Sappho, Gertrude Stein, Djuna Barnes, Adrienne Rich, Mary Daly, Monique Wittig, and others. This preface contains, as well, a certain number of biographical annotations recounting guilt, humiliation, contempt, despair, joy, courage, revolt, and the eroticism of lesbians throughout time.

The book is blank; the preface sets us dreaming.

I know that lesbians don't look up at the ceiling when they're making love, but one day I looked up and saw revealed to me the most beautiful fresco ever seen by women – on my lesbian word of honour. It was perfectly real, this fresco, and at the bottom of it was written: a lesbian who does not reinvent the world is a lesbian in the process of disappearing.

"Lesbiennes d'écriture" was presented in Vancouver at the Women and Words conference in June of 1983. It appeared in *Women and Words: An Anthology* (Vancouver: Harbour, 1985).

...
the poem if tournament tempts me
absent line
abstracts me even closer to you
in order to bring itself
about
at the outer edge of lips, the poem be/
comes inseparable from everyday reality
from the moment there is decision
to make a sign with the hand lights the temples

an image is a state of the soul
between women
a state of the soul is an image

<u>*lesbian*</u>

Excerpt from the poem "Tempes" in
Dont j'oublie le titre

ACCESS TO WRITING:
RITES OF LANGUAGE

WHEN I USE THE EXPRESSION "access to writing," clearly I imply that writing is desirable. For I know that writing is memory, power of presence, and proposition. I also know that the act of writing permits me to exist within and beyond my biographical constraints. For in writing I become *everything*: subject, characters and narrative, hypothesis, discourse and certitude, metaphor and movement of thought. In writing, I become a process of mental construction which enables me to synthesize that which in life – real life – must be portioned out to fiction and to reality. In writing, I can foil all the laws of nature and I can transgress all rules, including those of grammar. I know that to write is to bring oneself into being; it is *like* determining what exists and what does not, it is *like* determining reality.

I say all that using the "I." Now, let us imagine this "I" in the masculine plural repeating its truth throughout the centuries as though it were the Truth. Let's imagine that this masculine plural, better known as Man, takes up, in all its splendour, all its mediocrity, with all its fears and ecstasies, the entire field of semantics and the imaginary. Let's imagine that in all its glorious pride, this masculine plural "I" has effectively taken up all significant space in the order he himself has conceived. Let's imagine the worst, that in one fell swoop of spirit and pen, he has crossed out Woman's existence, decreed the inferiority of females, and invented THE woman. Then let us imagine the magnitude of the imagination we will require to understand, articulate, and disseminate the quintessential image that we, women, want of ourselves in terms of our presence in the world.

Roland Barthes writes in *Writing Degree Zero*[1] that "writing is an act of historical solidarity." One can then understand the "emotional problem" that access to writing represents to a woman. For one who writes cannot desert language's memory. To write, one must, desiring subject, want to assert one's presence in language, actualizing with the aid of this language, a manner of being (style), a way of seeing (vision), and a system of thinking (order).

I would like, first of all then, bearing in mind the memory already inscribed in language, to examine the antonyms which lodge themselves at the heart of the semantic unity which constitutes "Woman," antonyms which paralyze women's imaginative capacities, both discursive and desiring; antonyms from which is derived the permanent state of double-bind and contradiction in which women live.

SHE: HER ABSENCE / HER PRESENCE (THE IMAGE)

For centuries, women have learned to become familiar with words and stock phrases whose magic is to render them, at one and the same time, invisible, fatally present, and usefully real.

Invisible: Where there is Man, there are *no women.* The moment a woman transcends what is thought to be her nature, that is to say, when she is at her best, she, it is said, becomes like a man. This is gender erasure. Woman at her

---

1. Roland Barthes, *Writing Degree Zero,* trans. Richard Miller (New York: Hill and Wang, 1967), p. 14.

best is invisible as woman. Man, as "symbol of universal
wholeness, as centre of the world of symbols,"[2] produces an
effect of presence and precedence in each man, effects a plen-
itude which constitutes simultaneously his humanity and his
superiority. Where there is humanity, woman is invisible. To
dispel the invisibility of Woman, whose meaning and presence we intuit in ourselves like a motif of identity, is one task
of writing which necessitates that we make sense slip and
move in ways hitherto unheard of in language's imaginary.

Fatally Present: Where woman is invisible, that is, in the
symbolic field, we still find, however obliquely, her menacing
presence, for she is decidedly there, like life and death. Sirens,
witches, Gorgons, fairies, nymphs are all fatally present in
each woman like an evil power leading men to their ruin.

Usefully Real: Since women cannot be eliminated, this species which disgraces the whole of humanity might as well be
used, to the extent that it can be. Women who are "usefully
real" represent quite simply the actual presence of women in
everyday life and the uses to which they are put. Mothers,
wives, and whores, all assigned to maintenance work. Figures, roles, models, frozen in the tautology of daily reality.
Realist imagery: Man-made "Woman," suspended over our
heads like a constant threat to our lives, and living inside us
like a vexatious habit.

You will have noted that I've mentioned neither the ama-
zon nor the lesbian; essential figures, to be sure — carriers of
women's pride, initiators of women's autonomy, and above
all, figures animated by the keen presence of woman. Amazons and lesbians are the only women not invented by Man.
In this sense, they are figures both utopian and damned,
figures to whom access is forbidden, exactly like writing,
which I earlier described as desirable.

---

2. Jean Chevalier and Alain Gheerbrandt, *Dictionnaire des symboles*
   (Paris: Robert Laffont, 1969).

CONQUEST OF
THE IMAGE AS RETORT

Thus the magic of words, as practiced in the context of the patriarchal imagination, serves *at one and the same time*:

1. to exclude women from representation, when they surpass the limits of what is prescribed for them; that is, when they become subjects in their own right – they are assimilated into Man;
2. to reintegrate women into representation as threatening and deadly enemies. Powerful, nevertheless;
3. to scorn and ridicule the exploited alienated face women put on in the exploited alienated day-to-day reality;
4. to promote the value of this same everyday life.

This game of "Now you see them / Now you don't" is synchronized to the point where it is nearly impossible to catch hold of a positive image of "woman" and it is particularly impossible to linger there long enough to bring it into focus, that is, to grasp the Idea. Insofar as we are able with difficulty to catch sight of the positive image there at the limits of the subliminal, we can state that in each woman the belief that such an image exists alternates between minimal certainty and maximum doubt.

Therein is found the perceptual irresoluteness in a woman's consciousness regarding the existence of the positive image; it becomes a source of hesitation, which here must be understood to contain both "to have scruples and to look for one's words."

It is in finding the words – and nowhere as in writing does one look so hard for one's words – that a woman initiates herself into that positive image which makes her exist as subject.

This image is both motif and motive. This image is captivating, like an emotion which enthusiastically invests itself in the consciousness to which it is disposed.

This image makes sense of the sense we give to words. Words move the way of our desire and our desire is two-fold: while it is inclined toward the positive image, it also expresses regret at the absence of this image from the symbolic field. For desire – which extends itself toward the potentially present positive image, seeking to reach it as *subject* – must, in the process, lament the absence of this positive image, that is, it will want to lodge a complaint in language for this inconceivable absence. This is the desire of *retort*.[3]

THE UNTENABLE
DISCURSIVE POSTURE

My intention here is to show the difficulties of the discursive posture in which all women find themselves, including those aware of the imposture and the lie of the patriarchy. I use the word *posture* which describes an attitude, bearing, a position which is said to be "hardly natural" or "hardly suitable," keeping in mind all the while that posture is a way of holding oneself in a certain position, a hold, this meaning, among other things, to hold for true, "to be composed of coherent elements which entail what is probable."

When everything conspires (individuals, language, and society) to deny your perceptions, that is, the primary infor-

---

3. *Translator's Note.* In the original text, this sentence – "C'est le désir de la réplique." – functions on three levels: the desire to be able to retort, i.e. to disprove or refute; the desire to replicate the positive image entailed in woman as subject; and the desire inherent in the text of the retort.

mation from which it is possible to state something with conviction (whether to assert something definitively or to pro-
nounce something true), how does one *not* have self-doubts;
how does one avoid foundering in incoherence, ambiguity, or
contradiction? How does one elude paradox?

I recall here three of Paul Watzlawick's fundamental vari-
ants of paradox in *How Real is Real?*:[4]

1. If an individual is punished for a correct perception of
   the outside world or of himself by a significant other, he
   will learn to distrust the data of his senses.
2. If an individual is expected by a significant other to have
   feelings different from those he actually experiences, he
   will eventually feel guilty for being unable to feel what
   he is told he ought to feel in order to be approved of by
   the other person.
3. If a significant other gives injunctions that both demand
   and prohibit certain actions, a paradoxical situation
   arises in which the individual can obey only by disobey-
   ing.

If we look at the implications of the double bind for discourse, what we conclude is that the subject placed in a
double-bind situation can only stammer, lie, and contradict
itself.

The very place where the masculine subject demonstrates
his expertise in professing anything and everything – what he
knows and what he believes he knows – that is, the place
where the familiar presence of the masculine-neuter subject
renders his imaginative, creative, reductive or contradictory
contributions plausible, likely, even incontestable; precisely
there is the feminine subject repressed in the paradox of her

---

4. Paul Watzlawick, *How Real is Real? Communication, Disinformation,
   Confusion* (New York, Toronto: Random House, 1976), pp. 18-19.

symbolic absence and her real presence. Thus, wherever a woman believes she has found herself in language, without being there, she makes a mistake of reasoning. She is misled, and she misleads (sense). For how can she claim to be present where she truly is not? At most, she can only make it look like she is there by appearing to be there; she can only mis / take herself for someone else; a masculine other.

To discourse within a system of thought which denies her, the feminine subject undermines her thinking, her desire, and her hope.

INCREDIBLE SUBJECT / FABULOUS SUBJECT

Language is what permits us to put mental image on the route toward thought. The writing of fiction is what permits us to outmanoeuvre "straight" (linear-binary) language and thought.

We have said that at the origin of the feminine subject is this positive image of woman, and that this image yields desire. We have also stated that the feminine subject, confronted with the discourse which denies it, becomes improbable and incoherent; that in wanting to lance a retort, its hope is eroded. An inadmissible subject, the feminine subject seems to be real only in the fiction-writing which brings her about. In effect, it is in this realm (fiction) where ordinary sense is continually distorted, frustrated, disappointed, tricked, and misled by the style (the manner of speaking), that the test of meaning can truly take place. And it is there where one finds the "referential illusion,"[5] that, theoretically, we women traverse opaque

---

5. This is the title of an article by Michael Riffaterre in *Columbia Review*, 57, No. 2, (Winter 1978).

semantic reality, and in fiction that the "fabulous" unreal sub-ject we are becomes operative.

"Fabulous" subject, operative subject, such is the gist of what takes form as a result of our presence in writing. And that which in life escapes us, here doesn't escape us at all. So it is that in writing we work at the proposition which predicates our existence.

IT'S GETTING LATE

It's getting late. It's time to come back to the reality of this con-ference hall. What is real is a fabulous subject that haunts our three-dimensional lives. It's getting late for writing our place in history for history is like a hidden vice, always behind us. An accomplished pretense.

It's also getting late for recounting; yet each woman should – at least once in her life – recount her story with spirited, pas-sionate hope.

It's getting late. That's often what we say at dawn ... and then behold, our entire presence starts to be like a body in preparation for the magic of life, just like in reality. There are words for that. Still.

"Accès à l'écriture: rituel langagier" was presented at the "VIIIe Col-loque interdisciplinaire de la Société de philosophie québécoise" at the University of Montreal in November 1984. Another translation appeared in *Trivia,* No. 8 (Spring 1986).

In starting with the word woman in relation to utopia, M.V. had chosen to concentrate on an intuited abstraction. From the moment M.V. used the expression, the generic body, I knew that behind her the screen would be lowered and she would be projected into my universe.

Her only choice would be to consent. To consent is visibly the only verb which here could allow for verisimilitude, the transparency of utopian silk (in my universe, utopia would be a fiction from which would be born the generic body of she who thinks). I wouldn't have to have a first woman give birth to another woman. I would have in mind only the idea that she could be the one through whom anything can happen. I would have her to imagine while writing her, an abstract woman who would slip herself into my text, bearing fiction from so far that from afar, this woman with the properties of words, she would have to be seen coming. Infinitely virtual, formal in every dimension of knowledge, of method, and of memory. In fiction, I wouldn't have to invent her. Fiction would be the thread trailing the arrival of thought. Precisely the term.

Wandering and so much that of a woman. Brain — — — — — — — memory. At night, numbers and letters. When the equation comes to terms, I would rise up.

Picture Theory

INTERCEPTING
WHAT'S REAL

REALITY IS A FAMILIAR idea which appears obvious. Reality absolves one from one's consciousness; it is our "clear conscience" which justifies our daily acts. At the very beginning of our lives, reality is the part of our lives we learn by heart: it is the metonymy which takes the place of memory, vision, and sense. Women's reality is not men's reality. What is reality? Part of reality is in books. What is writing?

For whoever is made into a minority (I'm thinking here of women), and for whoever makes themselves marginal (I'm thinking here of writers, men and women), *reality* and *its* literature are intolerable. Only writing, thought of as a machine capable of helping us resolve problems of sense, puts us in a position where we think we are able to produce truth, that is, reality. Reality is always true, like something obvious, a three-dimensional certitude deep in the brain. It is language which renders reality approximate and chronological, and which consequently makes it subject to transformation. In return, we make use of writing in order to rediscover the obvious, lost in the multiplicities of sense and the contours of language.

◊

Writing is a tool which enables us to reflect, and to reflect on, the ways thought is organized. Just as the telescope and the microscope are tools which extend our sight beyond its actual possibilities, writing is a mechanism through which we can observe some of the sequences our brain develops in its potential/actual perception of energized matter. To write is to proceed to bring together the visible and the invisible, to make the obvious take shape. It is no accident that we say we are captivated by writing, for literally we are taken with its function, which is to help us capture the laws that govern the reality of our thinking/desiring being.

The mental processes we subscribe to while we write are the same as those which prevail while we think. As a result, we construct our texts in the same manner as we construct our vision of reality. Thought follows a course which escapes us. The text bears witness to observable repetitions which rhetoric identifies as figures: figures of speech, or tropes, and structural figures. Discourse bears witness to these same figures. But the processes of thought and those of writing escape us still. In this regard, we mask our ignorance by saying, "That's just her way of thinking" or "It's her style of writing," causing thought and writing to revert to a subjectivity. Subjectivity is not to be found in processes, only in content and strategies, that is, in the stylistic devices we use to accommodate our subjectivity.

◊

When we think, there is nothing which says we must slow down. When we write, we are necessarily slowed down by the act of forming letters or of striking the keys on a keyboard. The time this takes appears to be minimal, and for this reason we do not take it into account. But in terms of nanoseconds, this time constitutes space. It is in this continuum unknown to us that we intercept actuality, that is, the obvious. In this space, we are in a weightless state and, as such, we are freed up from gravity, from the body's capacity to fall, from the usual sensations of the senses, from ambivalence and from contradiction. When we leave this continuum, we have the memory of what was obvious. Our words are then charged with this memory, and we have the sensational sensation of sense. In a state of gravity, however, words no longer resemble what actually is; they seem fictive. We experience a strange effect then, which fascinates us. We begin all over again, fascinated by writing and, at the same time, misled by the text.

◊

While the function of writing may not be to mislead, it is nonetheless the function of the text. Writing is a manifestation of thought in its effort to succeed at getting closer to what is obvious. The text misleads sense, that is, text is "a trickster" or, if you prefer, it "seduces by an engaging appearance of reality." The more a text tricks the sense of what we have learned by heart in our lives, the more it seduces, captivates, the more it brings us closer to writing.

The text forbids us actuality, that is, it dis/claims the obvious, all the while leaving signs that it is, in fact, the result of a quest in this direction. It is because it dis/claims the obvious that text is not obvious at the highest level, the level of writing.

◊

Writing is a delay of reality to the extent that it reflects reality. When we write, time delays to which we are submitted translate themselves in the text as figures. Each figure is a relay centre, a transmission device. We read in the relay. In fact, we participate in the relay, as if at an abundant feast of sense, for sense figures in the relay; it evokes image. Thus we participate in the emotion of figures that are familiar to us, each as much

151

one as the other: a mother, a metaphor, a great love, an inversion, a childhood, an ellipsis. Emotion is the figure which moves within us.

"Intercepter le réel" is the text of a lecture given at the Forum des femmes, organized by *La Nouvelle Barre du Jour* on April 21, 1985. This text appeared in *La Nouvelle Barre du Jour*, No. 172 (March 1986).

It takes a minimum of concentration not to set fire to one's page. I am in quest and in combat. I nurture my archetypes of the future. This combat is thought and the elucidation of what thinks it. Appearances, facts, are important to me to the extent that I try to trace them to their origins, the fiction which makes them exist and emerge. The way you assemble reality from all its pieces. Like a child's Lego set, except I know that certain pieces are missing, that certain others are invisible to the naked eye, and that still others are magnified a thousand times in my mind and all around me. It looks like I amplify the reality of how things look. Reality is an apparent truth which is foiled by an actual text. And so as I stroll peacefully along the streets of a city, I examine but one aspect of reality, one aspect of text, which is, my reaction to the universe. Reality is an exhaustive response which never ceases to display itself before our eyes, like a fictive text which stirs up all the questions one could possibly imagine.

Journal intime

CERTAIN WORDS

AMID THE WORST possible misfortunes, the most daring nights of adoration, tragic death, and the softest skin, by the shores of all seas, and clothed in a utopian body and ecstasies, we proceed along the relief of words, agile among the sharp coral of l'Isla de las Mujeres. Dressed in a woman's body, patiently we mark time at the edge of the page; we are awaiting a feminine presence. With wet fingers, we turn the pages. We are waiting for truth to break through.

From one reading to another, words relay back and forth as though to test our endurance around an idée fixe, around the few self-images we have, images which apply to us only in the fictive space of our particular version of reality. From one reading to another, we fabulate stories from our desire, which is to identify what inspires us and what plunges us into such a state of "indescribable" fervour.

When this fervour comes over us, we say we are captivated by our reading and we advance slowly / rapidly toward our destiny. Our destiny is like a project, a life woven into us by innumerable lines; some are called the lines of the hand holding the volume. These lines innervate our entire body, like the logic of thought derived from the senses. Engrossed in our reading, we become aware of (being) the cause and the origin of the faces and landscapes surrounding us for we make allusion to them as one does to childhood, a desire, an inclination. Engrossed in our reading, we hear murmurs, entreaties, cries; we hear our voice looking for its horizon.

In our reading, there are mauves, some indigo, terrible looks, women adorned in jewels and silence. Bodies, sorely tried. Stirring visions. We open and close our eyes on them in the hope of a sonorous sequence, or a vital discussion perhaps. Our fervour sweeps into the text in order that from the discussion, truth might break through.

Amid the rhetoric, the logic of the senses, the paradoxes, and the sensation of becoming, we advance through our intention of forms. Sometimes, in the middle of the night, we might wake to re-read a passage, to see again the women we desire. And as we read it over, in our breast is an "indescribable" sensation which keeps us awake until dawn. At dawn, our spirit is extravagant; it wanders freely in forbidden zones and we have no choice but to explore them. I've heard that some women write at dawn, when they are in this state. I've heard that sometimes they burst into tears.

"I know the rhythms of the voice; I know how it jumps about. I know the experience and the adventure of the gaze." Toward this we soar with each reading, incredulous before truth, which, like a memory of shadow and of fervour, bursts in on us.

The words we notice speak to us and they fill us with unrest and pleasure. These words are revelations, enigmas, address. We transform them by an unconscious method, yet our consciousness finds itself enlightened by the process. Women reading, we become the allusion and the tone of a text.

What animates us in a sentence or an expression is a decision to be it. Inclined to become one with the text in order to seize in the fire of the action the brilliant exploit of our desire, we are astonished before the unanimity forming within us. Each intense reading is a beam of action.

Amid the equations, the pivotal axes, the intoxicating audacity, and the light which criss-crosses over us, we advance in our reading the way in theory we become what we desire. We advance toward a subtle and complex woman who reflects the process of our thinking and its forms of development. Words are one way to devour the desire which devours us with comparisons, taking us to the place where we become the appetite of knowledge and the knowledge of consciousness.

When we turn the pages with our wet fingers, going from terror to ecstasy, we confront eternity; we are believers and disbelieving before the sum total of bodies, craniums, orgasms; we confront the beyond of the whole and become desire's precision in the unrecountable space of the brain.

Truly, the sensational effect of reading is a feeling we cannot express, unless we underline. *With each reading, the intimacy of eternity is an intrigue we invent.* All reading, every reading, is a desire for image, an intention to re / present, which gives us hope.

"Certain mots" appeared in the journal *Tessera*, No. 2, *La Nouvelle Barre du Jour*, No. 157 (Sept. 1985).

BY THE SAME AUTHOR

POETRY

"Aube à la saison" in *Trois*, Montreal, L'A.G.E.U.M., 1965

Mordre en sa chair, Montreal, L'Estérel, 1966

L'écho bouge beau, Montreal, L'Estérel, 1968

Suite logique, Montreal, L'Hexagone, 1970

Le Centre blanc, Montreal, d'Orphée, 1970

Mécanique jongleuse, Paris, Génération, 1973

Mécanique jongleuse, followed by *Masculin grammaticale*, Montreal, L'Hexagone, 1974

La Partie pour le tout, Montreal, L'Aurore, "Lecture en vélocipède" collection, 1975

Le Centre blanc, Montreal, L'Hexagone, "Rétrospective" collection, 1978

D'arcs de cycle la dérive, poem, engraving by Francine Simonin, Saint-Jacques-le-Mineur, La Maison, 1979

Amantes, Montreal, Les Quinze, "Réelles collection," 1980

Double Impression, Montreal, L'Hexagone, Rétrospective collection, 1984

L'Aviva, Montreal, NBJ, 1985

Domaine d'écriture, Montreal, NBJ, 1985

Mauve with Daphne Marlatt, Montreal, NBJ, "Transformance" collection, 1985

Character/Jeu de lettres with Daphne Marlatt, Montreal, NBJ, "Transformance" collection, 1986

Sous la langue/Under Tongue, bilingual, trans. Susanne de Lotbinière-Harwood, Montreal, L'Essentielle and Ragweed Press, 1987

Dont j'oublie le titre, Marseille, Ryôan-ji, 1987

PROSE

Un livre, Montreal, du Jour, 1970, Les Quinze, 1980

Sold/out, Montreal, du Jour, 1973, Les Quinze, "Présence" collection, 1980

French kiss, Montreal, du Jour, 1974, Les Quinze, "Présence" collection, 1980

L'Amèr ou *Le Chapitre effrité*, Montreal, Le Quinze, 1977

Le Sens apparent, Paris, Flammarion, "Textes" collection, 1980

Picture theory, Montreal, Nouvelle Optique, "Fiction" collection, 1982

Journal intime, Montreal, Les Herbes rouges, 1984

Le Désert Mauve, Montreal, L'Hexagone, 1987

DRAMA

"L'écrivain," in *La Nef des sorcières*, Montreal, Les Quinze, 1976

ESSAYS

La Lettre aérienne, Montreal, Remue-Ménage, 1985

TRANSLATIONS

A Book (Un Livre), trans. Larry Shouldice, Toronto, Coach House Press, 1976

Turn of a Pang (Sold/Out), trans. Patricia Claxton, Toronto, Coach House Press, 1980

Daydream Mechanics (Mécanique jongleuse), trans. Larry Shouldice, Toronto, Coach House Press, 1980

These Our Mothers or: *The Disintegrating Chapter (L'Amèr),* trans. Barbara Godard, Toronto, Coach House Press, 1983

Lovhers (Amantes), trans. Barbara Godard, Montreal, Guernica Press, 1986

French Kiss (French kiss), trans. Patricia Claxton, Toronto, Coach House Press, 1986

La Lettre aérienne, trans. Luisa Murero, Rome, Felina Libri (forthcoming)

Marlene Wildeman and Nicole Brossard